Sarah Morgan

THE PRINCE'S WAITRESS WIFE

International Billionaires

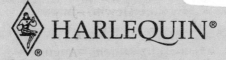

HARLEQUIN®

TORONTO • NEW YORK • LONDON
AMSTERDAM • PARIS • SYDNEY • HAMBURG
STOCKHOLM • ATHENS • TOKYO • MILAN • MADRID
PRAGUE • WARSAW • BUDAPEST • AUCKLAND

Recycling programs
for this product may
not exist in your area.

ISBN-13: 978-0-373-12798-6
ISBN-10:   0-373-12798-7

THE PRINCE'S WAITRESS WIFE

First North American Publication 2009.

Copyright © 2008 by Harlequin Book S.A.

Special thanks and acknowledgment are given to Sarah Morgan for her contribution to this work.

www.eHarlequin.com

Printed in U.S.A.

HARLEQUIN® Presents

Welcome to the February 2009 collection of Harlequin Presents!

This month read the final installment of Lynne Graham's trilogy VIRGIN BRIDES, ARROGANT HUSBANDS, *The Spanish Billionaire's Pregnant Wife.* Leandro Marquez ruthlessly stops at nothing to wed Molly when he discovers she's pregnant with his child! And don't miss the first part of our fabulous new series INTERNATIONAL BILLIONAIRES, which starts when shy, hardworking Holly is swept off her feet by the magnificent Prince Casper in Sarah Morgan's *The Prince's Waitress Wife.* Expect emotions to reach fever pitch in Carole Mortimer's *The Mediterranean Millionaire's Reluctant Mistress* when tycoon Alejandro is determined to claim his secret baby and possess Brynne in the process. And will an innocent plain Jane convince Sheikh Tair Al Sharif to let go of his mistrustful nature in Kim Lawrence's *Desert Prince, Defiant Virgin?* Business tycoon Santos Cordero is intent on seducing Alexa into a marriage of convenience in Kate Walker's *Cordero's Forced Bride,* while sexual tension heightens when Stefano seeks revenge after being left at the altar in Kate Hewitt's *The Italian's Bought Bride.* Be prepared for a battle of the sexes in Robyn Grady's *Confessions of a Millionaire's Mistress* as Celeste and Ben find they want the same thing in the bedroom…but different things from life! Plus, look out for Nicola Marsh's *The Boss's Bedroom Agenda,* in which a sizzling night spent together between Beth and her gorgeous new boss, Aidan, changes everything!

We'd love to hear what you think about Harlequin Presents. E-mail us at Presents@hmb.co.uk, or join in the discussions at www.iheartpresents.com and www.sensationalromance.blogspot.com, where you'll also find more information about books and authors!

All about the author...
Sarah Morgan

SARAH MORGAN was born in Wiltshire and started writing at the age of eight, when she produced an autobiography of her hamster.

At the age of eighteen she traveled to London to train as a nurse in one of London's top teaching hospitals, and she describes those years as extremely happy and definitely censored!

She worked in a number of areas after she qualified, but her favorite was the accident-and-emergency department, A&E, where she found the work stimulating and fun. Nowhere else in the hospital environment did she encounter such good teamwork between doctors and nurses.

By now her interests had moved on from hamsters to men, and she started writing romance fiction.

Her first completed manuscript, written after the birth of her first child, was rejected by Harlequin, but the comments were encouraging, so she tried again. On the third attempt her manuscript *Worth the Risk* was accepted unchanged. She describes receiving the acceptance letter as one of the best moments of her life, after meeting her husband and having her two children.

Sarah still works part-time in a health-related industry and spends the rest of the time with her family, trying to squeeze in writing whenever she can. She is an enthusiastic skier and walker, and loves outdoor life.

CHAPTER ONE

'KEEP your eyes down, serve the food and then leave. No lingering in the President's Suite. No gazing, no engaging the prince in conversation, and no flirting. *Especially* no flirting— Prince Casper has a shocking reputation when it comes to women. Holly, are you listening to me?'

Holly surfaced from a whirlpool of misery long enough to nod. 'Yes,' she croaked. 'I'm listening, Sylvia.'

'Then what did I just say?'

Holly's brain was foggy from lack of sleep and a constant roundabout of harsh self-analysis. 'You said—you told me—' Her voice tailed off. 'I don't know. I'm sorry.'

Sylvia's mouth tightened with disapproval. 'What is the matter with you? Usually you're extremely efficient and reliable, that's why I picked you for this job!'

Efficient and reliable.

Holly flinched at the description.

Another two flaws to add to the growing list of reasons why Eddie had dumped her.

Apparently oblivious to the effect her words were having, Sylvia ploughed on. 'I shouldn't have to remind you that today is the most important day of my career—catering for royalty at Twickenham Stadium. This is the Six Nations championship! The most important and exciting rugby tournament of the year! The eyes of the world are upon us! If we get this right, we're made. And more work for me means more work for you. *But I need you to concentrate!*'

A tall, slim waitress with a defiant expression on her face stalked over to them, carrying a tray of empty champagne glasses. 'Give her a break, will you? Her fiancé broke off their engagement last night. It's a miracle she's here at all. In her position, I wouldn't even have dragged myself out of bed.'

'He broke off the engagement?' Sylvia glanced from one girl to the other. 'Holly, is Nicky telling the truth? Why did he do that?'

Because she was efficient and reliable. Because her hair was the colour of a sunset rather than a sunflower. Because she was prudish and inhibited. Because her bottom was too big…

Contemplating the length of the list, Holly was swamped by a wave of despair. 'Eddie's been promoted to Marketing Director. I don't fit his new image.' So far she hadn't actually cried and she was quite proud of that—proud and a little puzzled. *Why hadn't she cried?* She *loved* Eddie. They'd planned a future together. 'He's expected to entertain clients and journalists and, well, he's driving a Porsche now, and he needs a woman to match.' With a wobbly smile and a shrug, she tried to make light of it. 'I'm more of a small family-hatchback.'

'You are much too good for him, that's what you are.' Nicky scowled and the glasses on the tray jangled dangerously. 'He's a b—'

'Nicky!' Sylvia gave a shocked gasp, interrupting Nicky's insult. 'Please remember that you are the face of my company!'

'In that case you'd better pay for botox before I develop permanent frown-lines from serving a bunch of total losers every day.' Nicky's eyes flashed. 'Holly's ex and his trophy-blonde slut are knocking back the champagne like Eddie is

Marketing Director of some Fortune 100 company, not the local branch of Pet Palace.'

'She's with him?' Holly felt the colour drain from her face. 'Then I can't go up there. Their hospitality box is really close to the President's Suite. It would just be too embarrassing for everyone. All his colleagues staring at me—*her* staring at me—what am I going to do?'

'Replace him with someone else. The great thing about really unsuitable men is that they're not in short supply.' Nicky thrust the tray into the hands of her apoplectic boss and slipped her arm through Holly's. 'Breathe deeply. In and out—that's it—good. Now, here's what you're going to do. You're going to sashay into that royal box and kiss that sexy, wicked prince. If you're going to fall for an unsuitable man, at least make sure he's a rich, powerful one. The king of them all. Or, in this case, the prince. Apparently he's a world-class kisser. Go for it. Tangling tongues at Twickenham. *That* would shock Eddie.'

'It would shock the prince, too.' Giggling despite her misery, Holly withdrew her arm from her friend's. 'I think one major rejection is enough for one week, thanks. If I'm not thin and blonde enough for the Managing Director of Pet Palace, I'm hardly going to be thin and blonde enough to attract a playboy prince. It's not one of your better ideas.'

'What's wrong with it? Straight from one palace to another.' Nicky gave a saucy wink. 'Undo a few buttons, go into the President's Suite and flirt. It's what I'd do.'

'Fortunately she isn't you!' Sylvia's cheeks flushed with outrage as she glared at Nicky. 'And she'll keep her buttons fastened! Quite apart from the fact I don't pay you girls to flirt, Prince Casper's romantic exploits are getting out of hand, and I've had strict instructions from the Palace—no pretty waitresses. No one likely to distract him. *Especially* no blondes. That's why I picked you in the first place, Holly. Red hair and freckles—you're perfect.'

Holly flinched. Perfect? *Perfect for melting into the background*.

She lifted a hand and touched her unruly red hair, dragged into submission with the liberal use of pins. Then she thought of what lay ahead and her battered confidence took another dive. The thought of walking into the President's Suite made her shrink. 'Sylvia—I really don't want to do this. Not today. I just don't feel—I'm having—' What—a bad hair day? A fat day? Frankly it was a battle to decide which of her many deficiencies was the most pronounced. 'They're all going to be thin, blonde, rich and confident.' *All the things she wasn't*. Her hands shaking, Holly removed the tray of empty glasses from her boss's hands. 'I'll take these back to the kitchens. Nicky can serve the royal party. I don't think I can stand them looking at me as if I'm—'

As if I'm nothing.

'If you're doing your job correctly, they shouldn't be looking at you at all.' Unknowingly echoing Holly's own thoughts, Sylvia removed the tray from her hands so violently that the glasses jangled again. Then she thrust the tray back at Nicky. '*You* take these glasses back to the kitchens. Holly, if you want to keep this job, you'll get up to the President's Suite right now. And no funny business. You wouldn't want to attract his attention anyway—a man in his position is only going to be interested in one thing with a girl like you.' Spotting another of the waitresses craning her neck to get a better view of the rugby players warming up on the pitch, Sylvia gave a horrified gasp. 'No, no. You're here to work, not gape at men's legs—' Abandoning Holly and Nicky, she hurried over to the other girl.

'Of course we're here to gape at men's legs,' Nicky

drawled. 'Why does she think we took the job in the first place? I don't know the first thing about scrums and line-outs, but I do know the men are gorgeous. I mean, there are men and there are men. And these are *men*, if you know what I mean.'

Not listening, Holly stared into space, her confidence at an all-time low. 'The wonder is not that Eddie dumped me,' she muttered, 'But that he got involved with me in the first place.'

'Don't talk like that. Don't let him do this to you,' Nicky scolded. 'Please tell me you didn't spend the night crying over him.'

'Funnily enough, I didn't. I've even been wondering about that.' Holly frowned. 'Perhaps I'm too devastated to cry.'

'Did you eat chocolate?'

'Of course. Well—chocolate biscuits. Do they count?'

'Depends on how many. You need a lot of biscuits to get the same chocolate hit.'

'I ate two.'

'Two biscuits?'

Holly blushed. 'Two packets.' She muttered the words under her breath and then gave a guilty moan. 'And I *hated* myself even more afterwards. But at the time I was miserable and *starving*! Eddie took me out to dinner to break off the engagement—I suppose he thought I might not scream at him in a public place. I knew something was wrong when he ordered a starter. He never orders a starter.'

'Well, isn't that typical?' Nicky's mouth tightened in disapproval. 'The night he breaks up with you, he finally allows you to eat.'

'The starter was for him, not me.' Holly shook her head absently. 'I can't eat in front of Eddie anyway. The way he watches me always makes me feel like a pig. He told me it was over in between the grilled fish and dessert. Then he dropped me home, and I kept waiting, but I just couldn't cry.'

'I'm not surprised. You were probably too hungry to summon the energy to cry,' Nicky said dryly. 'But eating chocolate biscuits is good news.'

'Tell that to my skirt. Why does Sylvia insist on this style?' Gloomily, Holly smoothed the tight black skirt over her hips. 'I feel as though I'm wearing a corset, and it's *so* short.'

'You look sexy as sin, as always. And eating chocolate is the first phase in the healing process, so you've passed that stage, which is a good sign. The next stage is to sell his ring.'

'I was going to return it.'

'Return it? Are you mad?' The empty glasses rattled again as Nicky's hands tightened on the tray. 'Sell it. And buy a pair of gorgeous shoes with the proceeds. Then you'll spend the rest of your life walking on his memory. And, next time, settle for sex without emotion.'

Holly smiled awkwardly, too self-conscious to confess that she hadn't actually had sex with Eddie. And that, of course, had been her major drawback as far as he was concerned. He'd accused her of being inhibited.

She bit back a hysterical laugh.

A small family-hatchback with central locking.

Would she be less inhibited if her bottom were smaller?

Possibly, but she wasn't likely to find out. She was always promising herself that she'd diet, but going without food just made her crabby.

Which was why her clothes always felt too tight.

At this rate she was going to die a virgin.

Depressed by that thought, Holly glanced in the direction of the President's Suite. 'I really don't think I can face this.'

'It's worth it just to get a look at the wicked prince in the flesh.'

'He hasn't always been wicked. He was in love once,'

Holly murmured, momentarily distracted from her own problems. 'With that Italian supermodel. I remember reading about them. They were the golden couple. Then she died along with his brother in that avalanche eight years ago. Horribly sad. Apparently he and his brother were really close. He lost the two people he loved most in the world. A family torn apart. I'm not surprised he's gone a bit wild. He must have been devastated. He probably just needs someone to love him.'

Nicky grinned. 'So go up there and love him. And don't forget my favourite saying.'

'What's that?'

'If you can't stand the heat…'

'Get out of the kitchen?' Holly completed the proverb but Nicky gave a saucy wink.

'Remove a layer of clothing.'

Casper strolled down the steps into the royal box, his handsome face expressionless as he stared across the impressive stadium. Eighty-two thousand people were gradually pouring into the stands in preparation for the breathlessly awaited match that was part of the prestigious Six Nations championship.

It was a bitterly cold February day, and his entourage was all muttering and complaining about freezing English weather.

Casper didn't notice.

He was used to being cold.

He'd been cold for eight long years.

Emilio, his Head of Security, leaned forward and offered him a phone. 'Savannah for you, Your Highness.'

Without turning, Casper gave an almost imperceptible shake of his head and Emilio hesitated before switching off the phone.

'Another female heart broken.' The blonde shivering next to him gave a disbelieving laugh. 'You're cold as ice, Cas.

Rich and handsome, admittedly, but very inaccessible emotionally. Why are you ending it? She's crazy about you.'

'That's why I'm ending it.' His voice hard, Casper watched the players warming up on the pitch, ignoring the woman gazing longingly at his profile.

'If you're ditching the most beautiful woman in the world, what hope is there for the rest of us?'

No hope.

No hope for them. No hope for him. The whole thing was a game, Casper thought blankly. A game he was sick of playing.

Sport was one of the few things that offered distraction. But, before the rugby started, he had to sit through the hospitality.

Two long hours of hopeful women and polite conversation.

Two long hours of feeling nothing.

His face appeared on the giant screens placed at either end of the pitch, and he watched himself with detached curiosity, surprised by how calm he looked. There was a loud female cheer from those already gathered in the stands, and Casper delivered the expected smile of acknowledgement, wondering idly whether any of them would like to come and distract him for a few hours.

Anyone would do. He really didn't care.

As long as she didn't expect anything from him.

He glanced behind him towards the glass windows of the President's Suite where lunch would be served. An exceptionally pretty waitress was checking the table, her mouth moving as she recited her checklist to herself.

Casper studied her in silence, his eyes narrowing slightly as she paused in her work and lifted a hand to her mouth. He saw the rise and fall of her chest as she took a deep breath— watched as she tilted her head backwards and stared up at the ceiling. It was strange body language for someone about to serve lunch.

And then he realised that she was trying not to cry.

Over the years he'd taught himself to recognise the signs of female distress so that he could time his exit accordingly.

With cold detachment he watched her struggle to hold back the oncoming tide of tears.

She was a fool, he thought grimly, *to let herself feel that deeply about anything*.

And then he gave a smile of self-mockery. Hadn't he done the same at her age—in his early twenties, when life had seemed like an endless opportunity, hadn't he naively allowed his emotions freedom?

And then he'd learned a lesson that had proved more useful than all the hours spent studying constitutional law or international history.

He'd learned that emotions were man's biggest weakness, and that they could destroy as effectively as the assassin's bullet.

And so he'd ruthlessly buried all trace of his, protecting that unwanted human vulnerability under hard layers of bitter life experience. He'd buried his emotions so deep he could no longer find them.

And that was the way he wanted it.

Without looking directly at anyone, Holly carefully placed the champagne-and-raspberry torte in front of the prince. Silver cutlery and crystal glass glinted against the finest linen, but she barely noticed. She'd served the entire meal in a daze, her mind on Eddie, who was currently entertaining her replacement in the premium box along the richly carpeted corridor.

Holly hadn't seen her, but she was sure she was pretty. Blonde, obviously. And not the sort of person whose best friend in a crisis was a packet of chocolate biscuits.

Did she have a degree? Was she clever?

Holly's vision suddenly blurred with tears, and she blinked frantically, moving slowly around the table, barely aware of the conversation going on around her. Oh dear God, she was going to lose it. Here, in the President's Suite, with the prince and his guests as witnesses. It was going to be the most humiliating moment of her life.

Trying to pull herself together, Holly concentrated on the dessert in her hand, but she was teetering on the brink. Nicky was right. She should have stayed in bed and hidden under the duvet until she'd recovered enough to get her emotions back under control. But she needed this job too badly to allow herself the luxury of wallowing.

A burst of laughter from the royal party somehow intensified her feelings of isolation and misery, and she placed the last dessert on the table and backed away, horrified to find that one of the tears had spilled over onto her cheek.

The release of that one tear made all the others rush forward, and suddenly her throat was full and her eyes were stinging.

Oh, please, no. Not here.

Instinct told her to turn around, but protocol forbade her from turning her back on the prince, so she stood helplessly, staring at the dusky pink carpet with its subtly intertwined pattern of roses and rugby balls, comforting herself with the fact that they wouldn't notice her.

People never noticed her, did they? She was the invisible woman. She was the hand that poured the champagne, or the eyes that spotted an empty plate. She was a tidy room or an extra chair. But she wasn't a *person*.

'Here.' A strong, masculine hand passed her a tissue. 'Blow.'

With a gasp of embarrassment, Holly dragged her horrified gaze from those lean bronzed fingers and collided with eyes as dark and brooding as the night sky in the depths of winter.

And something strange happened.

Time froze.

The tears didn't spill and her heart didn't beat.

It was as if her brain and body separated. For a single instant, she forgot that she was about to make a giant fool of herself. She forgot about Eddie and his trophy blonde. She even forgot the royal party.

The only thing in her world was this man.

And then her knees weakened and her mouth dried because he was *insanely* handsome, his lean aristocratic face a breathtaking composition of bold masculine lines and perfect symmetry.

His dark gaze shifted to her mouth, and the impact of that one searing glance scorched her body like the hottest flame. She felt her lips tingle and her heart thumped against her chest.

And that warning beat was the wake-up call she needed.

Oh, God. 'Your Highness.' Was she supposed to curtsy? She'd been so transfixed by how impossibly good-looking he was, she'd forgotten protocol. What was she supposed to do?

The unfairness of it was like a slap across the face. The one time she absolutely did *not* want to be noticed, she'd been noticed.

By Prince Casper of Santallia.

Her horrified gaze slid back to the tissue in his hand. And he *knew* she was upset. There was no hiding.

'Breathe,' he instructed in a soft voice. 'Slowly.'

Only then did she realise that he'd positioned himself right in front of her. His shoulders were wide and powerful, effectively blocking her from view, so that the rest of his party wouldn't see that she was crying.

The problem was, she could no longer remember *why* she'd felt like crying. One sizzling glance from those lazy dark eyes and her mind had been wiped.

Shrinking with embarrassment, but at the same time

relieved to have a moment to compose herself, Holly took the tissue and blew her nose. Despair mixed with fatalistic acceptance as she realised that she'd just given herself a whole new problem.

He was going to complain. And who could blame him? She should have smiled more. She should have paid attention when the bored-looking blonde seated to his right had asked her whether the goat's cheese was organic.

He was going to have her fired.

'Thank you, Your Highness,' she mumbled, pushing the tissue into her pocket. 'I'll be fine. Just don't give me sympathy.'

'There's absolutely no chance of that. Sympathy isn't my thing.' His gorgeous eyes shimmered with sardonic humour. 'Unless it's sympathy sex.'

Too busy holding back tears to be shocked, Holly took another deep breath, but her white shirt couldn't stand the pressure and two of her buttons popped open. With a whimper of disbelief, she froze. As if she hadn't already embarrassed herself enough in front of royalty, she was about to spill out of her lacy bra. Now what? Did she draw attention to herself and do up the buttons, or did she just hope he hadn't noticed…?

'I'm going to have to complain about you.' His tone was gently apologetic and she felt her knees weaken.

'Yes, Your Highness.'

'A sexy waitress in sheer black stockings and lacy underwear is extremely distracting.' His bold, confident gaze dropped to her full cleavage and lingered. 'You make it impossible for me to concentrate on the boring blonde next to me.'

Braced for an entirely different accusation, Holly gave a choked laugh. 'You're joking?'

'I never joke about fantasies,' he drawled. 'Especially sexual ones.'

He thought the blonde was boring?

'You're having sexual fantasies?'

'Do you blame me?' The frank appraisal in his eyes was so at odds with her own plummeting opinion of herself, that for a moment Holly just stared up at him. Then she realised that he *had* to be making fun of her because she knew she wasn't remotely sexy.

'It isn't fair to tease me, Your Highness.'

'You only have to call me Your Highness the first time. After that, it's "sir".' Amused dark eyes slid from her breasts to her mouth. 'And I rather think you're the one teasing *me*.' He was looking at her with the type of unapologetic masculine appreciation that men reserved for exceptionally beautiful women.

And that wasn't her. She knew it wasn't. 'You haven't eaten your dessert, sir.'

He gave a slow, dangerous smile. 'I think I'm looking at it.'

Oh God, he was actually flirting with her.

Holly's legs started to shake because he was so, so attractive, and the way he was looking at her made her feel like a supermodel. Her shrivelled self-esteem bloomed like a parched flower given new life by a shower of rain. This stunningly attractive, handsome guy—this gorgeous, mega-wealthy prince who could have had any woman in the world—found her so attractive that he wanted to flirt with her.

'Cas.' A spoiled female voice came from behind them. 'Come and sit down.'

But he didn't turn.

The fact that he didn't appear willing or able to drag his gaze from her raised Holly's confidence another few notches. She felt her colour mount under his intense, speculative gaze, and suddenly there was a dangerous shift in the atmosphere. Trying to work out how she'd progressed from tears to tension in such a short space of time, Holly swallowed.

It was *him*, she thought helplessly.

He was just gorgeous.

And way out of her league.

Flirting was one thing, but he had guests hanging on his every word—glamorous women vying for his attention.

Suddenly remembering where she was and who he was, Holly gave him an embarrassed glance. 'They're waiting for you, sir.'

The smooth lift of one eyebrow suggested that he didn't understand why that was a problem, and Holly gave a weak smile. He was the ruling prince. People stood in line. They waited for his whim and his pleasure.

But surely his pleasure was one of those super-groomed, elegant women glaring impatiently at his broad back?

Her cheeks burning, she cleared her throat. 'They'll be wondering what you're doing.'

'And that matters because…?'

Envious of his indifference, she laughed. 'Well—because generally people care what other people think.'

'Do they?'

She gave an awkward laugh. 'Yes.'

'Do *you* care what other people think?'

'I'm a waitress,' Holly said dryly. 'I have to care. If I don't care, I don't get tips—and then I don't eat.'

The prince lifted one broad shoulder in a careless shrug. 'Fine. So let's get rid of them. What they don't see, they can't judge.' Supremely confident, he cast a single glance towards one of the well-built guys standing by the door and that silent command was apparently sufficient to ensure that he was given instant privacy.

His security team sprang into action, and within minutes the rest of his party was leaving the room, knowing looks from the men and sulky glances from the women.

Ridiculously impressed by this discreet display of authority, Holly wondered how it would feel to be so powerful that you could clear a room with nothing more than a look. *And how must it feel to be so secure about yourself that you didn't care what other people thought about your actions?*

Only when the door of the President's Suite closed behind them did she suddenly realise that she was now alone with the prince.

She gave a choked laugh of disbelief.

He'd just dismissed the most glamorous, gorgeous women she'd ever seen in favour of—*her*?

The Prince turned back to her, his eyes glittering dark and dangerous. 'So.' His voice was soft. 'Now we're alone. How do you suggest we pass the time?'

CHAPTER TWO

HOLLY'S stomach curled with wicked excitement and desperate nerves. 'Thank you for rescuing me from an embarrassing moment,' she mumbled breathlessly, desperately racking her brains for something witty to say and failing. She had no idea how to entertain a prince. 'I can't imagine what you must think of me.'

'I don't understand your obsession with everyone else's opinion,' he drawled. 'And at the moment I'm not capable of thinking. I'm a normal healthy guy, and every one of my brain cells is currently focused on your gorgeous body.'

Holly made a sound somewhere between a gasp and a laugh. Disbelieving, self-conscious, but hopelessly flattered, she stroked her hands over her skirt, looked at him and then looked towards the door. '*Those* women are beautiful.'

'Those women spend eight hours a day perfecting their appearance. That's not beauty—it's obsession.' Supremely sure of himself, he took possession of her hand, locking her fingers into his.

Holly's stomach curled with excitement. 'We're not supposed to be doing this. They gave me this job because they thought I wasn't your type.'

'*Major* error on their part.'

'They told me you preferred blondes.'

'I think I've just had a major shift towards redheads.' With a wicked smile, he lifted his other hand and carelessly fingered a strand of her hair. 'Your hair is the colour of a Middle Eastern bazaar—cinnamon and gold. Tell me why you were crying.'

Caught in a spin of electrifying, exhilarating excitement, Holly's brain was in a whirl. For a moment she'd actually forgotten about Eddie. If she told him that her boyfriend had dumped her, would it make her seem less attractive?

'I was—'

'On second thoughts, don't tell me.' Interrupting her, he lifted her hand, checking for a ring. 'Single?'

Detecting something in his tone but too dazed to identify what, Holly nodded. 'Oh yes, completely single,' she murmured hastily, and then immediately wanted to snatch the words back, because she should have played it cool.

But she didn't feel cool. She felt—*relieved that she'd left the engagement ring at home.*

And he was smiling, clearly aware of the effect he was having on her.

Before she could stop him, he pulled the clip out of her hair and slid his fingers through her tumbling, wayward curls. 'That's better.' Very much the one in control, he closed his fingers around her wrists and hooked her arms round his neck. Then he slid his hands down her back and cupped her bottom.

'Oh.' Appalled that he seemed to be focusing on all her worst features, Holly gave a whimper of embarrassment and fought the impulse to wriggle away from him. But it was too late to take avoiding action. The confident exploration of his hands had ensured he was already well acquainted with the contours of her bottom.

'*Dio*, you have the most fantastic body,' he groaned,

moulding her against the hard muscle of his thighs as if she were made of cling film.

He thought she was fantastic?

Brought into close contact with the physical evidence of his arousal, Holly barely had time to register the exhilarating fact that he really did find her attractive before his mouth came down on hers in a hungry, demanding kiss.

It was like being in the path of a lightning strike. Her body jerked with shock. Her head spun, her knees were shaking, and her attempt to catch her breath simply encouraged a still more intimate exploration of her mouth. Never in her life had a simple kiss made her feel like this. Her fingers dug into his shoulders for support and she gasped as she felt his hands slide *under* her skirt. She felt the warmth of his hands against her bare flesh above her stockings, and then he was backing her against the table, the slick, erotic invasion of his tongue in her mouth sending flames leaping around her body and a burning concentration of heat low in her pelvis.

He was kissing her as though this was their last moments on Earth—*as if he couldn't help himself*—and Holly was swept away on the pure adrenaline rush that came with suddenly being made to feel irresistible.

Dimly she thought, *This is fast, too fast.* But, even as part of her analysed her actions with a touch of shocked disapproval, another part of her was responding with wild abandon, her normal insecurities and inhibitions dissolved in a rush of raw sexual chemistry.

Control slipped slowly from her grasp.

When Eddie had kissed her she'd often found her mind wandering—on occasions she'd guiltily caught herself planning meals and making mental shopping lists—but with the prince the only coherent thought in her head was *Please don't let him stop*.

But she *had* to stop, didn't she?

She didn't do things like this.

What if someone walked in?

Struggling to regain some control, Holly gave a low moan and dragged her mouth from his, intending to take a step back and think through her actions. But her good intentions vanished as she gazed up at his lean, bronzed features, her resolve evaporating as she took in the thick, dark eyelashes guarding his impossibly sexy eyes. *Oh, dear God*—how could any woman say no to a man like this? And, if sheer masculine impact wasn't enough, the way he was looking at her was the most outrageous compliment she'd ever received.

'You're staring at me,' she breathed, and he gave a lopsided smile.

'If you don't want men to stare, stay indoors.'

Holly giggled, as much from nerves as humour. 'I am indoors.'

'True.' The prince lifted one broad shoulder in an unmistakeably Latin gesture. 'In which case, I can't see a solution. You'll just have to put up with me staring, *tesoro*.'

'You speak Italian?'

'I speak whichever language is going to get me the result I want,' he purred, and she gave a choked laugh because he was so outrageously confident and he made her feel beautiful.

Basking in warmth of his bold appreciation, she suddenly felt womanly and infinitely desirable. Blinded by the sheer male beauty of his features, and by the fact that this incredible man was looking at *her*, her crushed heart suddenly lifted as though it had been given wings, and her confidence fluttered back to life.

All right, so she wasn't Eddie's type.

But this man—*this incomparably handsome playboy prince who had his pick of the most beautiful women in the world*—found her irresistible.

'You're staring at me too,' he pointed out, his gaze amused as he slid his fingers into her hair with slow deliberation. 'Perhaps it would be better if we both just close our eyes so that we don't get distracted from what we're doing.'

'What *are* we doing?' Weak with desire, Holly could barely form the words, and his smile widened as he gently cupped her face and lowered his mouth slowly towards hers.

'I think it's called living for the moment. And kissing you is the most fantastic moment I've had in a long time,' he said huskily, his mouth a breath away from hers.

She waited in an agony of anticipation, but he didn't seem in a rush to kiss her again, and Holly parted her lips in expectation, hoping that he'd take the hint.

Why on earth had she stopped him?

With a faint whimper of desperation, she looked into his eyes, saw the laughter there and realised that he was teasing her.

'That isn't very kind, Your Highness.' But she found that she was laughing too and her body was on fire.

'I'm not kind.' He murmured the words against her mouth. 'I'm definitely not kind.'

'I couldn't care less—please…' She was breathless and trembling with anticipation. 'Kiss me again.'

Flashing her a megawatt smile of male satisfaction, the prince finally lowered his head and claimed her mouth with his. He kissed her with consummate skill, his touch confident and possessive as he drew every last drop of response from her parted lips.

Her senses were swamped, her pulse accelerating out of control. Holly was aware of nothing except the overwhelming needs of her own body. Her arms tightened around his neck and she felt the sudden change in him. His kiss changed from playful to purposeful, and she realised with a lurch of exhilarating terror that this wasn't a mild flirtation or a game of 'boy kisses girl'. Prince Casper was a sexually experienced man who knew what he wanted and had the confidence to take it.

'Maybe we should slow this down,' she gasped, sinking her fingers into the hard muscle of his shoulders to give extra support to her shaking knees.

'Slow works for me,' he murmured, sliding his hands over the curve of her bottom. 'I'm more than happy to savour every moment of your utterly delectable body, and the game hasn't started yet. Why rush?'

'I didn't exactly mean—oh—' her head fell back as his mouth trailed a hot, sensuous path down her throat 'I can't concentrate on anything when you do that—'

'Concentrate on *me*,' he advised, and then he lifted his head and his stunning dark eyes narrowed. 'You're shivering. Are you nervous?'

Terrified. Desperate. Weak with longing.

'I—I haven't actually done this before.' Her whispered confession caused him to still.

'Exactly what,' he said carefully, 'Haven't you done before?' He released his hold on her bottom and slid his fingers under her chin, forcing her to look at him, his sharply intelligent eyes suddenly searching.

Holly swallowed.

Oh God, he was going to walk away from her. If she told him the truth, this experienced, sophisticated, gorgeous man would let her go and she'd spend the rest of her life regretting it.

Was she really going to let that happen?

No longer questioning herself, she slid her arms back round his neck. She didn't know what was going on here, she had no idea why she was feeling this way, but she knew she didn't want it to stop. 'I meant that I've never done anything like this in such a public place.'

He lifted an eyebrow. 'We're alone.'

'But anyone could walk in.' She wished he'd kiss her again. Would he think she was forward if *she* kissed him? 'What would happen then?'

'They'd be arrested,' he said dryly, 'And carted off to jail.'

'Oh—' Reminded of exactly with whom she was dealing, Holly felt suddenly intimidated. Please, *please,* let him kiss her again. When he'd kissed her she'd forgotten he was a prince. She'd forgotten *everything*. Feeling as though she were standing on the edge of a life-changing moment, Holly gazed up at him and he gave a low laugh.

'You talk too much, do you know that? So—now what? Yes, or no?' He smoothed a rebellious strand of hair away from her flushed cheeks in a slow, sensual movement, and that meaningful touch was enough to raise her temperature several degrees.

He was giving her the choice.

He was telling her that, if he kissed her again, he was going all the way.

'Yes,' she whispered, knowing that there would be a price to pay, but more than willing to pay it. 'Oh, yes.'

If she'd expected her shaky encouragement to be met with a kiss, she was disappointed.

'If you want to slow things down,' he murmured against her throat, 'I suppose I could always eat the dessert that's waiting for me on the table.'

Holly gave a faint whimper of frustration, and then he lifted his head and she saw the wicked gleam in his eyes. 'You're teasing me again.'

'You asked me to slow down, *tesoro*.'

She was finding it hard to breathe. 'I've definitely changed my mind about that.'

'Then why don't you tell me what you want?' He gave a sexy, knowing smile that sent her body into meltdown.

'I want you to kiss me again.' *And not to stop.*

'Do you?' His head lowered to hers, thick lashes partially shielding the mockery in his beautiful eyes. 'You're not supposed to give me orders.'

'Are you going to arrest me?'

'Now, there's a thought.' He breathed the words against her mouth. 'I could clap you in handcuffs and chain you to my bed until I'm bored.'

Her last coherent thought was *Please don't let him ever be bored*, and then he lifted her, and the demands of his hands on her thighs made it impossible for her not to wrap her legs around his waist. There was the faint rattle of fine bone-china as he positioned her on the table, and only when she felt the roughness of his zip against the soft flesh of her inner thigh did she realise that he'd somehow manoeuvred her skirt up round her waist.

With a gasp of embarrassment, she grabbed at the skirt, but she felt the hard thrust of his body against hers.

'I *love* the stockings,' he groaned, his dark eyes ablaze with sexual heat as he scanned the lacy suspender-belt transecting her milky-white thighs.

Thighs that definitely weren't skinny.

The fragile shoots of her self-confidence withered and died under his blatant scrutiny, and Holly tugged ineffectually at the hem of her skirt, trying to cover herself. 'Sylvia insists on stockings,' she muttered, and then, 'Do you think you could stop looking at me?'

'No, I definitely couldn't,' he assured her, a laugh in his voice as he released his hold on her bottom, grasped her hands and anchored them firmly around his neck. 'Take a deep breath in for me.'

'Why?'

A wicked smile transformed his face from handsome to

devastating. 'Because I want you to undo a few more buttons without me having to move my hands again. I'm never letting go of your bottom.'

Hyper-sensitive to that particular subject, Holly tensed, only to relax again as she registered the unmistakeable relish with which he was exploring her body. 'You *like* my bottom?'

'I just want to lose myself in you. What's your secret— exercise? Plastic surgery?' He gave another driven groan, captured her hips and drew her hard against his powerful erection. 'What did you *do* to it?'

'I ate too many biscuits,' Holly muttered truthfully, and he gave a laugh.

'I love your sense of humour. And from now on you can expect to receive a box of your favourite kind of biscuits on a daily basis.'

Slightly stunned that he actually seemed to *love* her worst feature, and trying not to be shocked by his unashamed sexuality, Holly was about to speak when his mouth collided with hers again and sparks exploded inside her head. It was like being the centre piece at a fireworks display, and she gave a disbelieving moan that turned to a gasp as her shirt fell open and her bra slid onto her lap.

'Are these also the result of the famous biscuit-diet?' An appreciative gleam in his eyes, he transferred his attention from her bottom to her breasts. '*Dio*, you're so fantastic I'm not even *thinking* about anything else while I'm with you.'

Something about that comment struck a slightly discordant note in her dazzled brain. Before she could dissect his words in more detail, he dragged his fingers across one nipple and shockwaves of pleasure sliced through her body. Then he lowered his dark head and flicked her nipple with his tongue.

Tortured by sensation, Holly's head fell back. Inhibitions blown to the wind by his expert touch, driven to the point of explosion by his vastly greater experience, she knew she was completely out of control and didn't even care. She felt like a novice rider clinging to the back of a thoroughbred stallion.

The burning ache in her pelvis grew to unbearable proportions, and she ground herself against him with a whimper of need. Desperate to relieve the almost intolerable heat that threatened to burn her up, she dug her nails into his shoulders.

'Please—oh—please.'

'My pleasure.' His eyes were two narrow slits of fire, his jaw hard, streaks of colour highlighting his cheekbones as he scanned her flushed cheeks and parted lips. Then he flattened her to the table and came down over her, the muscles in his shoulders bunched as he protected her from his weight.

Feeling as though she'd been dropped naked onto a bonfire, Holly gave a low moan that he smothered with a slow, purposefully erotic kiss.

'You are the most delicious thing that has ever been put on my table, my gorgeous waitress,' he murmured, his desperately clever fingers reaching lower. The intimacy of his touch brought another gasp to her lips and the gasp turned to a low moan as he explored her with effortless skill and merciless disregard for modesty.

'Are you protected?' His husky question didn't begin to penetrate her dazed brain, and she made an unintelligible sound, her legs tightening around his back, her body arching off the table in an attempt to ease the fearsome ache he'd created.

His mouth came down on hers again and she felt his strong hands close around her hips. He shifted his position, tilted her slightly, and then surged into her with a decisive thrust that drew a disbelieving groan from him and a shocked gasp from Holly.

An explosion of unbelievable pleasure suddenly splintered into pain, and her sharp cry caused him to still instantly.

Pain and embarrassment mingled in equal measure and for

a moment Holly dug her nails hard into his shoulders, afraid to move in case moving made it worse. And then suddenly the pain was gone and there was only pleasure—dark, forbidden pleasure that beckoned her forwards into a totally new world. She moved her hips restlessly, not sure what she wanted him to do, but needing him to do *something*.

There was the briefest hesitation on his part while he scanned her flushed cheeks, then he surged into her again, but this time more gently, his eyes holding hers the whole time as he introduced her to an intimacy that was new to her. And it was pleasure such as she'd never imagined. *Pleasure that blew her mind.*

She didn't know herself—her body at the mercy of sensual pleasure and the undeniable skill of an experienced male.

Controlled by his driving thrusts, she raced towards a peak and then was flung high into space, stars exploding in her head as he swallowed her cries of pleasure with his mouth, and reached his own peak with a triumphant groan.

Gradually Holly floated back down to earth, aware of the harshness of his breathing and the frantic beating of her own heart. He'd buried his face in her neck, and Holly focused on his glossy dark hair with glazed vision and numb disbelief.

Had that really just happened?

Swamped by an emotion that she couldn't define, she lifted her hand and tentatively touched him, checking that he was real.

She felt an immediate surge of tension through his powerful frame and heard his sharp intake of breath. Then he lifted his head, stared down into her eyes.

To Holly it was the single most intimate moment of her life, and when he opened his mouth to speak her heart softened.

'The match has started,' he drawled flatly. 'Thanks to you, I've missed kick-off.'

* * *

Keeping his back to the girl, Casper stared blankly through the glass of the President's Suite down into the stadium, struggling to regain some measure of control after what had undoubtedly been the most exciting sexual encounter of his life.

On the pitch below, England had possession of the ball, but for the first time in his life he wasn't in his seat, watching the game.

Which was something else that he didn't understand.

What the hell was going on?

Why wasn't he rushing to watch the game?

And since when had he been driven to have raw, uncontrolled sex on a table with an innocent woman?

Innocent.

Only now was he realising that all the signs had been there. And he'd missed them. *Or had he ignored them?*

Either way, he was fully aware of the irony of the situation.

He'd had relationships with some of the world's most beautiful, experienced and sophisticated women, but none of them had made him feel the way she had.

This was possibly the first time he'd enjoyed uncomplicated, motiveless sex. Sex driven by sheer, animal lust rather than human ambition.

Yes, the girl had known he was a prince.

But he was experienced enough to know that she'd wanted him as a man.

Hearing the faint brush of clothing against flesh, he knew she was dressing. For once he was grateful for the iron self-control and self-discipline that had been drilled into him in his few years in the army, because that was the only thing currently standing between restraint and a repeat performance.

It must have been novelty value, he reflected grimly, his shoulders tensing as he heard her slide her feet into her shoes.

That was the only explanation for the explosive chemistry they shared.

Which left them where, precisely?

He turned to find her watching him, and the confusion in her beautiful green eyes turned to consternation as a discreet tap on the door indicated that his presence was required.

The girl threw an embarrassed glance towards the door and frantically smoothed her skirt over her thighs. It was obvious from the uneven line of buttons on her shirt that she'd dressed in a hurry, with hands that hadn't been quite steady. Her hair was still loose, spilling over her narrow shoulders like a fall of autumn leaves, a beacon of glorious colour that effectively announced their intimacy to everyone who saw her.

Focusing on her soft mouth, Casper felt a sudden urge to power her back against the table and lose himself in her incredible body one more time.

'They'll be waiting for you in the royal box.' Her husky voice cut through his disturbingly explicit thoughts, and she hesitated for a moment and then walked over to him.

'Y-your Highness—are you all right?'

Casper stared down into warm green eyes, saw concern there, and suddenly the urge not to let her go was almost painful. There was something hopeful and optimistic about her, and he sensed she hadn't yet discovered that life was a cold, hard place.

Her smile faltered as she studied the grim set of his features. 'I guess this is what you'd call a bit of an awkward moment. So—well—' she waved a hand '—I have to get back to work and you—well…' Her voice tailed off and her white teeth clamped her lower lip. Then she took a deep breath, closed the gap between them, stood on tiptoe and kissed him on the mouth. 'Thank you,' she whispered. 'Thank you for what you've given me.'

Caught by surprise, Casper stood frozen to the spot, enveloped by a warm, soft woman. She tasted of strawberries and summer and an immediate explosion of lust gripped his body.

So he wasn't dead, then, he thought absently, part of him removed from what was happening. *Some things he could still feel.*

And then he heard a massive cheer from the crowd behind him and knew instantly what had happened.

Not so innocent, he thought grimly. Not so innocent that she didn't know how to work the press to her advantage. She was kissing him in the window, in full view of the cameras covering the game and the crowd.

Cameras that were now focusing on them.

She might have been sexually inexperienced, but clearly that hadn't prevented her from having a plan.

Surprised that he was still capable of feeling disillusioned and furious with himself for making such an elemental mistake, Casper locked his fingers round her wrists and withdrew her arms from his neck.

'You can stop now. If you look behind me, I think you'll find that you've achieved your objective.'

Confusion flickered in her eyes and then her attention fixed on something behind him. 'Oh my God.' Her hand covered her mouth. 'H—how did you know?' Her voice was an appalled whisper and she glanced at him in desperate panic. 'They filmed me kissing you. And it's up on the giant screens.' Her voice rose, her cheeks were scarlet, and her reluctant glance towards the stadium ended in a moan of disbelief. 'They're playing it again and again. Oh God, I can't believe this—it looks as though I'm—and my hair is all over the place and my bottom looks *huge*, and—everyone is looking.'

His eyes on the pitch, Casper watched with cool detachment as his friend, the England captain, hit a post with a drop-goal attempt.

'More importantly, you just cost England three points.'

With cold detachment, he realised that he was now going to have to brief his security team to get her out of here, but before he could speak she gave him a reproachful look and sped to the door.

'Do *not* leave this room,' Casper thundered, but she ignored him, tugged open the door, slipped between two of his security guards and sprinted out of sight.

Unaccustomed to having his orders ignored, Casper stood in stunned silence for a few precious seconds and then delivered a single command to his Head of Security. 'Find her.'

'Can you give me her name, Your Highness?'

Casper stared through the door. 'No,' he said grimly. 'I can't.'

All he knew was that she clearly wasn't as innocent as he'd first thought.

Feeling nothing except a desperate desire to hide from the world, Holly sprinted out of the room, shrinking as she passed a television screen in time to overhear the commentator say, *'Looks like the opening score goes to Prince Casper.'*

Hurtling down the stairs, she ran straight into her boss, who was marching up the stairs towards the President's Suite like a general leading an invading army onto enemy territory.

'Sylvia.' Her breath coming in pants, Holly stared at the other woman in horrified silence, noticing the blaze of fury in her eyes and the tightness of her lips.

'How dare you?' Sylvia's voice shook with anger. 'How dare you humiliate me in this way? I picked you especially because I thought you were sensible and decent. And you have destroyed the reputation of my company!'

'No!' Horribly guilty, overwhelmed by panic and humiliation, Holly shook her head. 'They don't even know who I am, and—'

'The British tabloid press will have your name before you're out of the stadium,' Sylvia spat. 'The entire nation heard the commentator say "That's one girl who isn't lying back thinking of England". If you wanted sleazy notoriety, then you've got it.'

Holly flinched under the verbal blows, feeling as vulnerable as a little rowing boat caught in a heavy storm out at sea. *What had she done?* This wasn't a little transgression that would remain her private secret. This was—this was… 'Prince Casper has kissed lots of women,' she muttered. 'So it won't be much of a story—'

'You're a waitress!' Sylvia was shaking with anger. 'Of course it's a story!'

Holly stared at her in appalled silence, realising that she hadn't once given any thought to the consequences of what they were doing. She hadn't thought at all. It had been impulse, chemistry, intimacy; she bit back a hysterical laugh.

What was intimate about having your love life plastered on sixty-nine-metre screens for the amusement of a crowd of eighty-two thousand people?

She swallowed painfully. 'Sylvia, I—'

'You're fired for misconduct!'

Her world crumbling around her, Holly was about to plead her case when she caught sight of Eddie striding towards them, his face like a storm cloud.

Unable to take any more, Holly gasped another apology and fled towards the kitchens. Heart pounding, cheeks flaming, she grabbed her bag and her coat, changed into her trainers and made for the door.

Nicky intercepted her. 'Where are you going?'

'I don't know.' Feeling dazed, Holly looked at her help-lessly. 'Home. Anywhere.'

'You can't go home. It's the first place they'll look.' Brisk and businesslike, Nicky handed her a hat and a set of keys. 'Stick the hat on and hide that gorgeous hair. Then go to my flat.'

'No one knows who I am.'

'By now they'll know more about you than you do. Go to my flat, draw the curtains and don't answer the door to anyone. Have you got the money for a cab?'

'I'll take the bus.' Too shocked to argue, Holly obediently scooped her hair into a bunch and tucked it under the hat.

'No way.' Nicky stuffed a note in her hand. 'Get a taxi—and hope the driver hasn't seen the pictures on the screen. Come to think of it, sit with a hanky over your nose. Pretend you have a cold or something. Go, go, *go!*'

Realising that she'd set into motion a series of events that she couldn't control, Holly started to walk towards the door when Nicky caught her arm.

'Just tell me one thing,' she whispered, a wicked gleam in her eyes. 'The rumours about the prince's talents—are they true?'

Holly blinked. 'I—'

'That good, huh?' Nicky gave a slow, knowing smile. 'I guess that answers my question. Way to go, baby.'

Ruthlessly focusing his mind on the game, Casper watched as the England winger swerved round his opponent and dived for the corner.

The bored blonde gasped in sympathy. 'Oh no, the poor guy's tripped. Right on the line. Why is everyone cheering? That's *so* mean.'

'He didn't trip, he scored a try,' Casper growled, simmer-ing with masculine frustration at her inappropriate comment. 'And they're cheering because that try puts England level.'

'This game is a total mystery to me,' the girl muttered, her eyes wandering to a group of women at the back of the royal box. 'Nice shoes. I wonder where she got them? Are there any decent shops in this area?'

Casper blocked out her comments, watching as the England fly-half prepared to take the kick.

A hush fell over the stadium and Saskia glanced around her in bemusement. 'I don't understand any of this. Why is everyone so quiet? And why does that gorgeous guy keep staring at the ball and then the post? Can't he make up his mind whether to kick it or not?'

'He's about to take a very difficult conversion kick right from the touchline. He's concentrating.' Casper's gaze didn't shift from the pitch. 'And if you open your mouth again I'll have you removed.'

Saskia snapped her mouth shut, the ball snaked through the posts, the crowd roared its approval, and a satisfied Casper turned wearily to the fidgeting blonde next to him. 'All right. *Now* you can ask me whatever you want to know.'

She gave him a hopeful look. 'Is the game nearly over?'

Casper subdued a flash of irritation and resolved never again to invite anyone who didn't share his passion for rugby. 'It's half time.'

'So we have to sit through the whole thing again? Tell me again how you know the captain.'

'We were in the rugby team at school together.'

Clearly determined to engage him in conversation now that there was a pause in the game, Saskia sidled a little closer. 'It was very bad of you to kiss that waitress. You are a very naughty boy, Cas. She'll go to the newspapers, you know. That sort always do.'

Would she?

Casper stared blankly at the crowd, trying to blot out the

scent of her hair and the taste of her mouth—the softness of her deliciously rounded bottom as she'd lifted herself against him.

For a brief moment in time, she'd made him forget. And that was more than anyone else had ever done.

'Why does your popularity never dip?' Clearly determined to ingratiate herself, Saskia kept trying. 'Whatever you do, however scandalous you are, the citizens of Santallia still love you.'

'They love him because he's turned Santallia from a sleepy, crumbling Mediterranean country into a hub of foreign investment and tourism. People are excited about what's happening.' It was one of Casper's friends, Marco, who spoke, a guy in his early thirties who had studied economics with him at university and now ran a successful business. 'Santallia is *the* place to be. The downhill-ski race has brought the tourists to the mountains in the winter, and the yacht race does the same for the coast in the summer. The new rugby stadium is sold out for the entire season, and everyone is talking about the Grand Prix. As a sporting venue, we're second to none.'

Hearing his successes listed should have lifted his mood, but Casper still felt nothing.

He made no effort to take part in the conversation going on around him and was relieved when the second half started because it offered him a brief distraction.

'What Santallia really wants from you is an heir, Cas.' Saskia delivered what she obviously thought was an innocent smile. 'You can't play the field for ever. Sooner or later you're going to have to break your supermodel habit and think about the future of your country. Oh no, fighting has broken out on the pitch. They're all sort of locked together.'

Leaving it to an exasperated Marco to enlighten her, Casper watched as the scrum half put the ball into the scrum. 'That was never straight,' he murmured, a frown on his face as he glanced at the referee, waiting for him to blow the whistle.

'Did you read that survey that put you top of the list of most eligible single men in the world? You can have any woman you want, Cas.' Oblivious to the impact of her presence on their enjoyment, Saskia continued to pepper the entire second half with her inane comments, all of which Casper ignored.

'A minute of play to go,' Marco murmured, and Casper watched as England kept the ball among the forwards until the final whistle shrilled.

The crowd erupted into ecstatic cheers at the decisive England victory, and he rose to his feet, abruptly terminating Saskia's attempts to converse with him.

Responsibility pressing in on him, he strolled over to his Head of Security. 'Anything?'

'No, sir,' Emilio admitted reluctantly. 'She's vanished.'

'You found out her name?'

'Holly, sir. Holly Phillips. She's a waitress with the contract catering company.'

'Address?'

'I already sent a team to her home, sir. She isn't there.'

'But I'm sure the photographers are,' Cas said grimly, and Emilio nodded.

'Two rows of them, waiting to interview her. Prince and waitress—it's going to be tomorrow's headlines. You want her to have protection?'

'A woman who chooses to kiss me in full view of television cameras and paparazzi doesn't need my protection.' Casper spoke in a flat, toneless voice. 'She knew exactly what she was doing. And now she's lying low because being unavailable will make it look as though she has something to hide. And having something to hide will make her story more valuable.'

She'd used him.

Casper gave a twisted smile. *And he'd used her, too, hadn't he?*

Emilio frowned. 'You think she did it to make money, sir?'

'Of course.' She'd actually had the temerity to thank him for what he'd given her! At the time he'd wondered what she meant, but now it was blindingly obvious.

He'd given her media opportunities in abundance.

He searched inside himself for a feeling of disgust or disillusionment. *Surely* he should feel something? Apparently she'd considered the loss of her virginity to be a reasonable price to pay for her moment of fame and fortune and that attitude deserved at least a feeling of mild disappointment on his part.

But disillusionment, disgust and disappointment all required expectations and, when it came to women, he had none.

Emilio was watching him. 'You don't want us to find her, Your Highness?'

Ruthlessly pushing aside thoughts of her soft mouth and delicious curves, Casper glanced back towards the pitch where the crowd was going wild. 'I think we can be sure that when she's ready she'll turn up. At this precise moment she's lying low, laughing to herself and counting her money.'

CHAPTER THREE

'YOU have *got* to stop crying!' Exasperated and concerned, Nicky put her arms round Holly. 'And—well—it isn't that serious, really.'

'Nicky, *I'm pregnant!* And it's the prince's baby.' Holly turned reddened eyes in her direction. 'How much more serious can it get?'

Nicky winced. 'Isn't it too soon to do a test? It could be wrong.'

'It isn't too soon. It's been over two weeks!' Holly waved a hand towards the bathroom. 'And it isn't wrong. It's probably still on the floor where I dropped it if you want to check, but it doesn't exactly give you a million options. It's either pregnant or not pregnant. And I'm *definitely* pregnant! Oh God, I don't believe it. Once—*once*—I have sex and now I'm pregnant. Some people try for *years*.'

'Yes, well, the prince is obviously super-fertile as well as super-good looking.' Nicky gave a helpless shrug, searching for something to say. 'You always said you couldn't wait to have a baby.'

'But *with* someone! Not on my own. I never, ever, wanted to be a single mother. It was the one thing I promised myself was never going to happen. It *really* matters to me.' Holly pulled another tissue out of the box and blew her nose hard. 'When I dreamed about having a baby, I dreamed about giving it everything I never had.'

'By which I presume you mean a father. God, your dad *really* screwed you up.' With that less than comforting comment, Nicky sank back against the sofa and picked at her nail varnish. 'I mean, how could anyone have a kid like you, so kind and loving, and then basically just, well, walk out? And you were seven—old enough to know you'd been rejected. And not even coming to find you after your mum died. I mean, for goodness' sake!'

Not wanting to be reminded of her barren childhood, Holly burrowed deeper inside the sleeping bag. 'He didn't know she'd died.'

'If he'd stayed in touch he would have known.'

'Do you mind if we don't talk about this?' Her voice high-pitched, Holly rolled onto her back and stared up at the ceiling. 'I have to decide what to do. I've lost my job, and I can't go home because the press are like a pack of wolves outside my flat. And the whole world thinks I'm a giant slut.' Dying of embarrassment, her insides twisting with regret, she buried her face in the pillow.

And she *was* a slut, wasn't she?

She'd had sex with a total stranger.

And not just sex—recklessly abandoned, wild sex. Sex that had taken her breath away and wiped her mind of guilt, worry, *morals*.

Whenever Eddie had touched her, her first thought had always been *I mustn't get pregnant*. When the prince had touched her the only thought in her head had been more, *more…*

What had happened to her?

Yes, she'd been upset and insecure about herself after her break up with Eddie, but that didn't explain or excuse it.

And then she remembered the way the prince had planted

himself protectively in front of her, shielding her from the rest of the group. What other man had ever shown that degree of sensitivity? He'd noticed she was upset, shielded her, and then…

Appalled with herself, she gave another moan of regret, and Nicky yanked the sleeping bag away from her.

'Stop torturing yourself. You're going to be a great mother.'

'How can I be a great mother? I'm going to have to give my baby to someone else to look after while I work! Which basically means that someone else will pick my baby up when it cries.'

'Well, if it's a real bawler that might be an advantage.'

Holly wiped the tears from her face with a mangled damp hanky. 'How can it be an advantage? I want to be there for my baby.'

'Well, perhaps you'll win the lottery.'

'I can't afford to play the lottery. I can't even afford to pay you rent.'

'I don't want rent, and you can sleep on my sofa as long as you need to.' Nicky shrugged. 'You can't exactly go home, can you? The entire British public are gagging for pictures of you. "Where's the waitress?" is today's headline. Yesterday it was "royal's rugby romp". Rumour has it that they're offering a reward to anyone who shops you. Everyone wants to know about that kiss.'

'For crying out loud.' Holly blew her nose hard. 'People in the world are starving and they want to write about the fact that I kissed a prince? Doesn't anyone have any sense of perspective?' *Thank goodness they didn't know the whole story*.

'Well, we all need a little light relief now and then, and people love it when royalty show they're human.' Nicky sprang to her feet. 'I'm hungry and there's no food in this flat.'

'I don't want anything,' Holly said miserably, too embarrassed to admit to her friend that the real reason she was so upset was because the prince hadn't made any attempt to get in touch.

Even though she knew it was ridiculous to expect him to contact her, a small part of her was still desperately hoping that he would. Yes, she was a waitress and he was a prince, but he'd liked her, hadn't he? He'd thrown all the other people out of the room so that he could be with *her*, and he'd said all those nice things about her, and then…

Holly's body burned in a rush of sexual excitement that shocked her. Surely after sex as mind-blowing as that, he might have been tempted to track her down?

But how could he get in touch when the press was staking out her flat? She had a mental image of the prince hiding behind a bush, waiting for the opportunity to bang on her door. 'Do you think he's really annoyed about the headlines?'

'Don't tell me you're worrying about *him*!' Nicky had her hand in a packet of cereal. 'He just pulls up his bloody drawbridge, leaving the enemy on the outside!'

Holly bit her lip. She was the one who'd kissed him by the window. *She'd had no idea.* 'I feel guilty.'

'Oh, please! This is Prince Casper we're talking about. He doesn't care what the newspapers write about him. *You're* the one who's going to suffer. If you ask me, the least he could have done was give you some security or advice. But he's left you to take the flak!'

Holly's spirits sank further at that depressing analysis. 'He doesn't know where I am.'

'He's a prince,' Nicky said contemptuously, flopping back down on the sofa, her mouth full of cereal. 'He commands a whole army, complete with special forces. He could find you in an instant if he wanted to. MI5, FBI, I don't know—one of that lot. One word from him and there'd be a satellite trained on my flat.'

Shrinking at the thought, Holly slid back into the sleeping bag. 'Close the blinds.' *What had she done?*

'Well, you can go on hiding if that's what you want. Or you could give those sharks outside your flat an interview.'

'Are you mad?'

'No, I'm practical. Thanks to His Royal Highness, you have no job and you're trapped indoors. Sell your story to the highest bidder. "My lunchtime of love" or "sexy Santallian stud"?'

Appalled, Holly shook her head. 'Absolutely not. I couldn't do that.'

'You have a baby to support.'

'And I don't want my child looking back at the year he was conceived and seeing that his life started with me dishing the dirt on his dad in the papers! I just want the whole thing to go away.'

It was ironic, she thought numbly, that she'd fantasised about this exact moment ever since she was a teenager. She'd *longed* to be a mother. Longed to have a child of her own—to be able to create the sort of family she'd always wanted.

She'd even lain awake at night, imagining what it must be like to discover that you were pregnant and to share that excitement with a partner. She'd imagined his delight and his pride. She'd imagined him pulling her into a protective hug and fiercely declaring that he would never leave his family.

Not once, ever, had she imagined that she'd be in this position, doing it on her own.

One rash moment, one transgression—*just one*—and her life had been blown apart. Even though she was in a state of shock, the deeper implications weren't lost on her. Her hopes of eventually being able to melt back into her old life unobserved died. She knew that once someone spotted that she was pregnant it wouldn't take long for them to do the maths.

This was Prince Casper of Santallia's child.

Nicky stood up. 'I need to buy some food. Back in a minute.' The front door slammed behind her, and moments later Holly heard the doorbell. Assuming Nicky had forgotten something, she slid off the sofa and padded over to the door.

'So this is where you've been hiding!' Eddie stood in the doorway, holding a huge, ostentatious bunch of dark-red roses wrapped in cheap cellophane.

Holly simply stared, suddenly realising that she'd barely thought about him over the past two weeks.

'I didn't expect to see you here, Eddie.'

He gave a benign smile. 'I expect it seems like a dream.' Sure of himself, Eddie smiled down at her. 'Aren't you going to invite me in?'

'No. You broke off our engagement, Eddie. I was devastated.' Holly frowned to herself. Her devastation hadn't lasted long, though, had it? It had been supplanted by bigger issues—but should that have been possible? Did broken hearts really mend that quickly?

'I can't talk about this on the doorstep.' He pushed his way into the flat and thrust the flowers into her hands. Past their best, a few curling petals floated onto the floor. 'Here. These are for you. To show that I forgive you.'

'Forgive me?' Holly winced as a thorn buried itself into her hand. Gingerly she put the flowers down on the hall table and sucked the blood from her finger. 'What are you forgiving me for?'

'For kissing the prince.' Eddie's face turned the same shade as the roses. 'For making a fool of me in public.'

'Eddie—you were the one partying in that box with your new girlfriend.'

'She was no one special. We both need to stop hurting each other. I admit that I was furious when I saw you kissing the prince, then I realised that it must have been hard on you, watching me get that promotion and then losing me. But it seems to have loosened up something inside you. A whole new you emerged.' He grinned like a schoolboy who had just discovered girls. 'You've always been quite shy and a bit prim. And suddenly you were, well, wild. When I saw you kissing him, I couldn't help thinking it should have been me.'

Looking at him, Holly realised that not once during her entire passionate episode with the prince had she thought 'this should have been Eddie'.

'I know you only did it to bring me to my senses,' Eddie said. 'And it worked. I see now that you are capable of passion. I just need to be more patient with you.'

The prince hadn't been patient, Holly thought absently. He'd been very *impatient*. Rough, demanding, forceful.

'I didn't kiss the prince to make you jealous.' She'd kissed him because she couldn't help herself.

'Never mind that now. Put my ring back on your finger, and we'll go out there and tell the press we'd had a row and you kissed the prince because you were pining for me.'

Life had a strange sense of humour, Holly reflected numbly. Eddie was offering to get back together. But she was already being propelled down a very different path.

'That isn't possible.'

'We're going to make a great couple.' He was smugly confident. 'We'll have the Porsche and the big house. You don't need to be a waitress any more.'

'I like being a waitress,' Holly said absently. 'I like meeting new people and talking to them. People tell you a lot over a cup of coffee.'

'But who wants to be weighed down with someone else's problems when you can stay at home and look after me?'

'It *can't* happen, Eddie—'

'I know it's like a fairy tale, but it *is* happening. By the way, the flowers cost a fortune, so you'd better put them in water. I need the bathroom.'

'Door on the right,' Holly said automatically, and then gave a gasp. 'No, Eddie, you can't go in there.' Oh, dear God, she'd left everything on the floor—he'd see.

Wanting to drag him back but already too late, she stood there, paralysed into inactivity by the sheer horror of the moment. The inevitability was agonising. It was like witnessing a pile-up—watching, powerless, as a car accelerated towards the back of another.

For a moment there was no sound. No movement.

Then Eddie appeared in the door, his face white. 'Well.' His voice sounded tight and very unlike himself. 'That certainly explains why you don't want to get back together again.'

'Eddie—'

'You're holding out for a higher prize.' Looking slightly dazed, he stumbled into the living room of Nicky's flat. Then he looked at her, his mouth twisted with disgust. 'A year we were together! And we never—you made we wait.'

'Because it didn't feel right,' she muttered, mortified by how it must look, and anxious that she'd damaged his ego. That was the one part of this whole situation that she hadn't even been able to explain to herself. Why had she held Eddie at a distance for so long and yet ended up half-naked on the table with Prince Casper within thirty minutes of meeting him? 'Eddie, I really don't—'

'You really don't *what*?' He was shouting now, his features contorted with rage as he paced across Nicky's wooden floor. 'You really don't know why you slept with him? Well I'll tell you, shall I? *You slept with him because he's a bloody prince!*'

'No—'

'And you've really hit the jackpot, haven't you?' He gave a bitter laugh. 'No wonder you weren't excited about my Porsche. I suppose he drives a bloody Ferrari, does he?'

Holly blinked. 'I have no idea what he drives, Eddie, but—'

'But it's enough to know you're getting a prince and a palace!'

'That isn't true. I haven't even decided what to do yet.'

'You mean you haven't decided how to make the most money out of the opportunity.' Eddie strode towards the door of her flat, scooping up the flowers on the way. 'I'm taking these with me. You don't deserve them. And you don't deserve *me*. Good luck in your new life.'

Holly winced as the flowers bashed against the door frame and flinched as he slammed the door.

A horrible silence descended on the flat.

A few forlorn rose petals lingered on the floor like drops of blood, and her finger stung from the sharp thorn.

She felt numb with shock. Awful. And guilty, because it was true that she'd shared something with the prince that she hadn't shared with Eddie.

And she didn't understand that.

She didn't understand any of it.

Two weeks ago she would have relished the idea of getting back together with Eddie.

Now she was just relieved that he'd gone.

Sinking onto Nicky's sofa, she tried to think clearly and logically.

There was no need to panic.

No one would be able to guess she was pregnant for at least four months.

She had time to work out a plan.

Flanked by four bodyguards, gripping a newspaper like a weapon, Casper hammered on the door of the fourth-floor flat.

'You didn't have to come here in person, Your Highness.' Emilio glanced up and down the street. 'We could have had her brought to you.'

'I didn't want to wait that long,' Casper growled. In the past few hours he'd discovered that he was, after all, still capable of emotion. Boiling, seething anger. Anger towards her, but mostly at himself, for allowing himself to be put in this position. What had happened to his skills of risk assessment? Since when had the sight of a delicious female body caused him to abandon caution and reason? Women had been throwing themselves in his path since he'd started shaving, but never before had he acted with such lamentable lack of restraint.

She'd set a trap and he'd walked right into it.

'I *know* she's in there. Get this door open.'

Before his security team could act, the door opened and she stood there, looking at him.

Prepared to let loose the full force of his anger, Casper stilled, diverted from his mission by her captivating green eyes.

Holly.

He knew her name now.

She was dressed in an oversized, pale pink tee-shirt with a large embroidered polar bear on the front. Her hair tumbled loose over her shoulders and her feet were bare. It was obvious that she'd been in bed, and she looked at him with shining eyes, apparently thrilled to see him. 'Your Highness?'

She looked impossibly young, fresh and naïve and Casper wondered again what had possessed him to get involved with someone like her.

She had trouble written across her forehead.

And then she smiled, and for a few seconds he forgot everything except the warmth of that smile. The anger retreated inside him, and the only thing in his head was a clear memory of her long legs wrapped around his waist. Casper gritted his teeth, rejecting the surge of lust, furious with himself, and at the same time slightly perplexed because he'd never in his life felt sexual desire for a woman dressed in what looked like a child's tee-shirt.

This whole scenario was *not* turning out the way he'd expected.

How could he still feel raw lust for someone who'd capsized his life like a boat in a storm? And why was she staring at him as if they were acting out the final scenes of a romantic movie? After the stunt she'd pulled, he'd expected hard-nosed negotiation.

'I see you didn't bother dressing for my visit.' Ignoring the flash of hurt in her eyes, he strode into the tiny flat without invitation, leaving his security team to ensure their privacy.

'Well, obviously I had no idea that you'd be coming.' She tugged self-consciously at the hem of her tee-shirt. 'It's been well over two weeks.'

Casper assessed the apartment in a single glance, taking in the rumpled sleeping bag on the sofa. *So this was where she'd been hiding.* 'I have a degree in maths. I know exactly how long it's been.'

Her eyes widened in admiration. 'You're good at maths? I always envy people who are good with numbers. Maths was never really my thing.' Colour shaded her cheeks. 'But I always had pretty good marks in English. I think I'm more of a creative person.'

At a loss to understand how the conversation had turned to school reports, Casper refocused his mind, the gravity of the situation bearing down on him. 'Do you have any idea what you've done?'

Biting her lip, she looked away for a few seconds, then met his gaze again. 'You're talking about the fact I kissed you in front of the window, aren't you?' Her glance was apologetic.

'It's probably a waste of time saying this, but I really *am* sorry. I honestly had no idea how much trouble that would cause. You have to remember I'm not used to the press. I don't know how they operate.'

'But you're learning fast.' Her attempt at innocence simply fed his irritation. He would have had more respect for her if she'd simply admitted what she'd done.

But no confession was forthcoming. Instead she gave a tentative smile. 'Well, I've been amazed by how persistent they are, if that's what you're saying. That newspaper you're holding—' she glanced at it warily '—is there another story today? I don't know how you stand it. Do you eventually just get used to it?'

Her friendliness was as unexpected as it was inappropriate, and Casper wondered what on earth she thought she was doing. Did she really think she could act the way she had and still enjoy civilised conversation?

The newspaper still in his hand, he strolled to the window of the flat and looked down into the street. How long did they have? By rights the press should already have found them. 'I've had people looking for you.'

'Really?' Her face brightened slightly, as if he'd just delivered good news. 'I sort of assumed— Well, I thought you'd forgotten about me.'

'It would be hard to forget about you,' he bit out, 'Given that your name has been in the press every day for the past fortnight.'

'Oh.' There was a faint colour in her cheeks, and disappointment flickered in her eyes, as if she'd been hoping for a different reason. 'The publicity is awful, isn't it? That's why I'm not at my flat. I didn't *want* them to find me.'

'Of course you didn't. That would have ruined everything, wouldn't it?' He waited for her to crumble and confess, but instead she looked confused.

'You sound *really* angry. I don't really blame you, although to be honest I thought you'd be used to all the attention by now. D-do you want to sit down or something, sir?' Stammering nervously, she swept the sleeping bag from the sofa, along with a jumper, an empty box of tissues and a pair of sheer black stockings that could have come straight from the pages of an erotic magazine. Bending over revealed another few inches of her impossibly long legs, and Casper's body heated to a level entirely inconsistent with a cold February day in London.

'I don't want to sit down,' he said thickly, appalled to discover that despite her sins all he really wanted to do was spread her flat and re-enact their last encounter.

Her gaze clashed with his and everything she was holding tumbled onto the floor. 'C—can I get you a drink? Coffee? It's just instant—nothing fancy—' Her voice was husky and laced with overtones that suggested coffee was the last thing on her mind. Colour darkened her cheeks and she dragged her gaze from his, clearly attempting to deny the chemistry that had shifted the temperature of the room from Siberian to scorching.

'Nothing.'

'No. I don't suppose there's much here that would interest you.' She tugged at the tee-shirt again. 'Sorry—this whole situation is a bit surreal. To be honest, I can't believe you're here. I mean, you're a prince and I'm—'

'Pinching yourself?'

'It is weird,' she confided nervously. 'And a bit awkward, I suppose.'

'Awkward?' Shocked out of his contemplation of her mouth by her inappropriate choice of adjective, Casper turned on her. 'We've gone way beyond *awkward*.' His tone was savage, and he saw her take several steps backwards. 'What were you thinking? What was going on in that manipulative female brain of yours? Was it all about making a quick profit? Or did you have an even more ambitious objective?'

The sudden loss of colour from her face made the delicate freckles on her nose seem more pronounced. 'Sorry?'

Casper slammed the newspaper front-page up onto the coffee table. 'I hope you don't live to regret what you've done.'

He watched as she scanned the headline, her soft, pink lips moving silently as she read: *Prince's Baby Bliss*. Then her eyes flew to his in startled horror. 'Oh, no.'

'Is it true?' The expression on her face killed any hope that the press had been fabricating the story to increase their circulation figures. 'You're pregnant?'

'Oh my God—how can they have found out? How can they possibly know?'

'Is it true?' His thunderous demand made her flinch.

'Yes, it's true!' Covering her face with her hands, she plopped onto the sofa. 'But this isn't how— I mean, I haven't even got my head round it myself.' Her hands dropped. 'How did they find out?'

'They rely on greedy people willing to sell sleaze.' The bite in his tone seemed to penetrate her shock, and she wrapped her arms around her waist in a gesture of self-protection.

'I take it from that remark that you think I told them. And I can see this looks bad, but—' She broke off, her voice hoarse. 'It wasn't me. Honestly. I haven't spoken to the press. Not once.'

'Then how do you explain the fact that the story is plastered over the front pages of every European newspaper? The palace press-office was inundated with calls yesterday from journalists wanting a comment on the happy news that I am at last to be a father.' He frowned slightly, disconcerted by her extreme pallor. 'You're very pale.'

'And that's surprising? Have you *read* that thing?' Her

voice rose. 'It's all right for you. You're used to this. Your face is always on the front of newspapers, but this is all new to me, and I hate it! My life doesn't feel like my own any more. *Everyone* is talking about me.'

'That's the usual consequence of selling your story to a national newspaper.'

But she didn't appear to have heard him. Her eyes were fixed on the newspaper as though he'd introduced a deadly snake into her flat.

'It must have been Eddie,' she whispered, her lips barely moving. 'He knew about the baby. He's the only one who could have done this.'

'You disgust me.' Casper didn't bother softening his tone, and shock flared in her green eyes.

'*I* disgust *you*?' She couldn't have looked more devastated if he'd told her that a much-loved pet had died. 'But you—I mean, we—'

'We had sex.' Casper delivered the words with icy cool, devoid of sympathy as yet another layer of colour fled from her cheeks. 'And you used that to your advantage.'

'Wait a minute—just slow down. How can any of this be to my advantage?' Gingerly she reached for the newspaper and scanned the story. Then she dropped it as though she'd been burned. 'This is *awful*. They know *everything*. Really private stuff, like my dad leaving home when I was seven and the fact I was taken into care, stuff I don't talk about.' Her voice broke. 'My whole life is laid out on the front page for everyone to read. And it's just *horrible*.' Her distress appeared to be genuine and Casper felt a flicker of exasperation.

'What exactly did you think would happen? That they'd only print nice stories about you? Nice stories don't sell newspapers.'

'*I didn't tell them!*' She rose to her feet, her tousled hair spilling over her shoulders. 'It *must* have been Eddie.'

'And what was his excuse? He didn't feel ready for father-hood? Was he only too eager to shift the responsibility onto some other guy?'

Puzzled, she stared at him for a moment, and then her mouth fell open. 'This isn't Eddie's baby, if that's what you're implying!'

'Really?' Casper raised an eyebrow in sardonic appraisal. 'Then you have been busy. Exactly how many men were you sleeping with a few weeks ago? Or can't you remember?'

Hot colour poured into her cheeks, but this time it was anger, not embarrassment. 'You!' Her voice shook with emotion and her eyes were fierce. 'You're the only man I was sleeping with. The only man I've *ever* slept with. And you know it.'

Casper remembered that shockingly intense and intimate moment when he'd been *sure* she was a virgin. Then he reviewed the facts. 'At the time I really fell for that one. But virgins don't have hot, frantic sex with a guy within moments of meeting him, *tesoro*. Apart from that major miscalculation on your part, you were pretty convincing.'

She lifted her hands to her burning face. 'That was the first time I'd ever—'

'Fleeced a billionaire prince?' Helpfully, Casper finished her sentence, and her eyes widened.

'You think I set some sort of trap for you? You think I *faked* being a virgin? For heaven's sake—what sort of women do you mix with?'

Not wanting to dwell on that subject, Casper watched her with cool disdain. 'I know this isn't my baby,' he said flatly. 'It isn't possible.'

'You mean because it was just the once.' She sank back onto the sofa, stumbling over the words. 'I know it's unlikely, but that's what's happened. And you might be a prince, but that doesn't give you the right to speak to me as though I'm—'

Unsure of herself, her eyes slid to the door, as if she were worried the security guards might arrest her for treason.

'What are you, Holly? What's the correct name for a woman who sleeps with a guy for money?'

Her body was trembling. 'I haven't asked you for money.'

'I'm sure what you earned from the newspapers will keep you and *Eddie* going for a while. What did you have planned—monthly bulletins to keep the income going? *Now* I understand why you thanked me.'

'Th—thanked you?'

'As you kissed me in the window.' His mouth curved into a cynical smile. 'You thanked me for what I'd given you.'

'But that was—' She broke off and gave a little shake of her head. 'I was feeling *really* low that day. The reason you walked over to me in the first place was because I was crying. And I thanked you because you made me feel good about myself. Nothing else. Up to that point in my life, I knew nothing about the way the media worked.'

'You expect me to believe that it's coincidence that you've been in hiding for over two weeks? You were holding out for the big one. The exclusive to end all exclusives.' He saw panic in her eyes and felt a flash of satisfaction. 'I don't think you have any idea what you've done.'

'What *I've* done? You were there, too! You were part of this, and I think you're being *totally* unfair!' Her hands were clasped by her sides, her fingers opening and closing nervously. 'I'm having *your* baby. Frankly, that in itself is enough to make me feel a bit wobbly, without you standing there accusing me of being a—a—' She choked on the word. 'And, as if that isn't bad enough, you're telling me you don't believe it's yours!'

'You want to know what I think?' His tone was the same temperature as his heart—icy cold. 'I think you were already pregnant when you turned on the tears and had sex with me on my table. That's why you were crying. I think you were panicking about how you'd cope with a baby on a waitress's salary. And you saw me as a lucrative solution. All you had to do was pretend to be a virgin, and then I wouldn't argue a paternity claim.'

'That's all rubbish! I had sex with you because—' She broke off and gave a hysterical laugh. 'I don't *know* why I had sex with you! Frankly the whole episode was pretty shocking.'

Their eyes collided, and shared memories of that moment passed between them like a shaft of electricity.

His eyes dropped to her wide, lush mouth and he found himself remembering how she'd tasted and felt. Even though he now realised that she couldn't possibly have been a virgin, he still wanted her with almost indecent desperation.

'*Stop* looking at me like that,' she whispered, and Casper gave a twisted smile, acknowledging the chemistry that held them both fast. Invisible chains, drawing them together like prisoners doomed to the same fate.

'You should be pleased I'm looking at you like that,' he drawled softly, 'Because good sex is probably the only thing we have going for us.'

Even as his mind was withdrawing, his hands wanted to reach out and haul her hard against him. He saw her eyes darken to deep emerald, saw her throat move as she murmured a denial.

'I honestly don't know what's going on here,' she muttered. 'But I think you'd better leave.'

Somehow her continuing claim at innocence made the whole episode all the more distasteful, and the face of another woman flashed into his brain—a woman so captivating that he'd been blind to everything except her extraordinary beauty. 'What sort of heartless bitch would lie about the identity of her baby's father?' Ruthlessly he pushed the memories down, his anger trebling. 'Don't you have a conscience?' His words sucked the last of the colour from her cheeks.

'Get out!' Her voice sounded strange. High pitched. Robotic. 'I don't care if you're a prince, just get out!' Her legs were shaking and her face was as white as an Arctic snowfield. 'I was *so* pleased to see you. That day when you comforted me when I was upset—I thought you were a really nice, decent person. A bit scary, perhaps, but basically nice. When I opened the door and saw you standing there I actually thought you'd come to see if I was OK—can you believe that? And now I feel like a complete fool. Because you weren't thinking about me. You were thinking about yourself. So just go! Go back to your palace, or your castle, or wherever it is you live.' The wave of her hand suggested she didn't care where he lived. 'And do whatever it is you want to do.'

'You've robbed me of that option.'

'Why? Even if the world does think I'm having your baby, *so what*? Don't tell me you're worried about your reputation. You're the playboy prince.' There was hurt in her voice, that same voice that only moments earlier had been soft and gentle. 'Since when has reputation mattered to you? When you have sex with a woman, everyone just smiles and says what a stud you are. I'm sure the fact that you've fathered a child will gain you some major testosterone points. Walk away, Your Highness. Isn't that what you usually do?'

'You just don't get it, do you?' His voice was thickened and raw. 'You have no idea what you've done.'

What exactly *had* she done?

Appalled, Holly stared at him.

The anger in his face was real enough. It was clear that he genuinely believed that he couldn't be the father of her baby. And her only proof was the fact that she'd been a virgin.

But he didn't believe her, did he?

And could she blame him for that? It was true that she hadn't behaved like a virgin. The entire encounter had been one long burst of explosive chemistry. It had been the only time in her life that she'd been out of control.

And that chemistry was back in the room, racking up the tension between them to intolerable levels, the electricity sparking between them like a live cable. His gaze dropped to her lips and she saw in his eyes that his mind was in exactly the same place as hers.

It was like a chain reaction. His glance, her heartbeat, harsh breathing—*her or him?*—and tension—tension like she'd never experienced before.

Streaks of colour accentuated his aristocratic cheekbones and he stepped towards her at exactly the same moment she moved towards him. The attraction was so fierce and frantic that when she heard a ringing sound she actually wondered whether an alarm had gone off.

Then she realised that it was the phone.

Hauling his gaze from hers, Casper inhaled sharply. '*Don't* answer that.'

Still reeling from the explosion of sexual excitement, Holly doubted she'd be capable of answering it even if she'd wanted to. Her legs were trembling and the rhythm of her breathing was all wrong.

She watched dizzily as he crossed the room and lifted a bunch of papers from the printer.

Mouth grim, shoulders tense, he leafed through them and then lifted his gaze to hers. 'What were you doing? Profiling your target?'

Having completely forgotten that she'd actually printed out some of the sheets on him, including a particularly flattering picture, Holly suddenly wished she could sink through the floor. 'I—I was looking you up.' What else could she say? She could hardly deny it, given that he was holding the evidence of her transgression in his hands.

'Of course you were.' He gave a derisive smile. 'I'm sure you wanted to know just how well you'd done. So, now we've cleared that up, let's drop the pretence of innocence, shall we?'

'OK, so I'm human!' Her face scarlet, her knees trembling, Holly ran damp palms over her tee-shirt, wishing she could go and change into something else. He looked like something out of a glossy magazine, and she was dressed in her most comfortable tee-shirt that dated back at least six years. 'I admit that I wanted to find out stuff about you. You were my first lover.'

'So you're sticking to that story.' He dropped the papers back onto the desk and Holly lifted her chin.

'It's *not* a story. It's the truth.'

'I just hope you don't regret what you've done when you have two hundred camera lenses trained on your face and the world's press yelling questions at you.'

She shrank at the thought. 'That isn't going to happen.'

'Let me tell you something about the life you've chosen, Holly.' Tall and powerfully built, he looked as out of place in her flat as a thoroughbred racehorse in a donkey derby. From the stylish trousers and long cashmere coat, to the look of cool confidence on his impossibly handsome face, everything about him shrieked of enormous wealth and privilege. 'Everywhere you go there will be a photographer stalking you, and most of the time you won't even know they're there until you see the picture next day. Everyone is going to want a piece of you, and that means you can no longer have friends, because even friends have their price and you'll never know who you can trust.'

'I don't need to hear this—'

'Yes, you do. You won't be able to smile without someone

demanding to know why you're happy and you won't be able to frown without someone saying that you're suffering from depression and about to be admitted to a clinic.' He hammered home the facts with lethal precision. 'You'll either be too thin or too fat—'

'Too fat, *obviously*.' Heart pounding, Holly sank down onto the sofa. 'Enough. You can stop now. I get the picture.'

'I'm describing your new life, Holly. The life you've chosen.'

There was a tense, electric silence and she licked her lips nervously. 'What are you saying?'

'You have made sure that the whole world believes that this is my baby. And, as a result, the whole world is now waiting for me to take appropriate action.'

Pacing back over to the window, he stared down into the street.

Holly had a sudden sick feeling in her stomach. 'A—appropriate action? What do you mean?'

There was a deathly silence and then he turned, his eyes empty of emotion. 'You're going to marry me, Holly.' The savage bite in his tone was a perfect match for the chill in his eyes. 'And you may think that I've just made your wildest dreams come true, but I can assure you that you're about to embark on your worst nightmare.'

CHAPTER FOUR

'So WHEN do you think he'll be back?' Holly paced across the priceless rug in the Georgian manor house. 'I mean, he's been gone for two weeks, Emilio! I haven't even had a chance to talk to him since that day at the flat.' *The day he'd announced that she was going to marry him.* 'Not that this house isn't fabulous and luxurious and all that—but he virtually kidnapped me!'

'On the contrary, His Highness was merely concerned for your safety,' Emilio said gently. 'The press had discovered where you were and the situation was about to turn extremely ugly. It was imperative that we extracted you from there as fast as possible.'

Remembering the crowd of reporters that had suddenly converged on Nicky's flat, and the slick security operation that had ensured their escape, Holly rubbed her fingers over her forehead. 'Yes, all right, I accept that, but that doesn't explain why he hasn't been in touch. When is he planning to come back? We need to *talk*.'

There was so much she needed to say to him.

When she'd opened the door to the flat and seen the prince standing there, her first reaction had been one of pure joy. For a crazy moment she'd actually thought that he was there because he'd spent the past two weeks thinking about her and decided that he needed to see her again. Her mind had raced forward, imagining all sorts of unrealistic scenarios that she was now too embarrassed to even recall. Her crazy, stupid brain had actually started to believe that extraordinary things *could* happen to someone ordinary like her.

And then he'd strode into her flat like a Roman conqueror neutralising the enemy.

Remembering everything he'd said to her, she felt a rush of misery.

He didn't believe it was his baby and the injustice of that still stung. True, she wasn't exactly proud of the way she'd behaved, but it seemed he'd conveniently forgotten his own role in the affair.

And as for his proposal of marriage—well, that unexpected twist had more than kept her mind occupied over the past two weeks.

Had he meant it? *Was he serious?* And, if he was serious, what was her response going to be?

It was the most difficult decision she'd ever had to make, and the arguments for and against had gone round and round in her head like a fairground carousel. Marrying him meant being with a man who didn't know her or trust her, but *not* marrying him meant denying her baby a father.

And that was the one thing she'd promised herself would never happen to any child of hers.

Reminding herself of that fact, Holly straightened her shoulders and stared across the beautifully landscaped gardens that surrounded the manor.

Their baby was *not* going to grow up thinking that his father had abandoned him. She swallowed down the lump that sprang into her throat. *Their baby was not going to be the only child in school not making a Father's Day card.*

Which meant that her answer had to be yes, regardless of everything else.

What else mattered? Hopefully over time the prince would realise how wrong he had been about her, and once the baby was born it would be a simple matter to prove paternity. Perhaps, then, their relationship could develop.

Realising that Emilio was still watching her, she felt a squeeze of guilt. 'I'm sorry. I'm being really selfish. Is there any news about your little boy? Have you phoned the hospital this morning?'

Remembering just how taciturn and uncommunicative the prince's Head of Security had been when they'd first met, she was relieved that he'd responded to her attempts to be friendly.

'His temperature is down,' he told her. 'And he's responding to the antibiotics, although they're still not sure what it was.'

'Your poor wife must be so tired. And little Tomasso must be missing you. I remember having chicken pox just after—' *Just after her father had left.* The feelings of abandonment were as fresh as ever and Holly walked across to him and touched his arm. 'Go home, Emilio,' she urged. 'Your wife would like the support and your little boy would dearly love to see his daddy.'

'That's out of the question, madam.'

'Why? I'm not going anywhere. I feel really guilty that you're stuck here with me. If it weren't for me, you'd be back home in Santallia.'

Emilio cleared his throat. 'If I may say so, your company has been a pleasure, madam. And you've been a great comfort since Tomasso was ill. I'll never forget your kindness that first night when he was first taken into hospital and you stayed up and kept me company.'

'I've never been thrashed so many times at poker in my life. It's a good job I don't have any money to lose,' Holly said lightly. 'The moment the prince turns up, you're going home.'

But what if he didn't turn up?

Perhaps he didn't want to marry her any more.

Perhaps he'd changed his mind.

Or perhaps he'd just imprisoned her here, away from the press, until the story died down? After all, he believed that she'd talked to the press. Was he keeping her here just to ensure her silence?

Her thoughts in turmoil, Holly spent the rest of the morning on the computer in the wood-panelled study that overlooked the ornamental lake. Resisting the temptation to do another trawl of the Internet for mentions of Prince Casper, she concentrated on what she was doing and then wandered down to the kitchen to eat lunch with the head chef and other members of the prince's household staff.

'Something smells delicious, Pietro.' Loving the cosy atmosphere of the kitchen, she warmed her hands on the Aga. Naturally chatty by nature, and delighted to find herself suddenly part of this close community, Holly had lost no time in getting to know everyone living and working in the historic manor house.

'It's a pleasure to cook for someone who enjoys her food, madam,' the chef said, smiling warmly as he gestured towards some pastries cooling on a wire rack. 'Try one and give me your verdict. You're eating for two, remember.'

'Well, I'd rather not be the size of two. I'm not sure I'm meant to be developing cravings this early, but already I don't think I can live without your *pollo alla limone*.' Holly still felt slightly self-conscious that everyone clearly felt so possessive about her baby. She bit into a pastry and moaned with genuine appreciation. 'Oh, please—this is *sublime*. Truly, Pietro. I've never tasted anything this good in my life before. What is it?'

Pietro blossomed. 'Goat's cheese, with a secret combination of herbs—' He broke off as Emilio entered the room and Holly smiled.

'Emilio, thank goodness.' She took another nibble of pastry. 'You're just in time to stop me eating the lot by myself.'

'Miss Phillips.' The bodyguard's eyes were misted, and Holly dropped the pastry, alarmed to see this controlled man so close to the edge.

'What? What? Has something happened? Did the hospital ring?'

'How can I ever thank you? You are—' Emilio's voice was gruff and he cleared his throat. 'A very special person. My wife called—she just received a delivery of beautiful toys. How you managed to arrange that so quickly I have no idea. Tomasso is thrilled.'

'He liked his parcel?' Relieved that nothing awful had happened, Holly retrieved the pastry and threw Pietro an apologetic glance. 'Sorry. Slight overreaction there on my part. Just in case you can't tell, I briefly considered drama as a career. So he liked the toys? I couldn't decide between the fire engine and the police car.'

'So you bought both.' Emilio shook his head. 'It was unbelievably generous of you, madam.'

'It was the least I could do given I'm the reason you're not with him.' Holly frowned and glanced towards the window. 'What's that noise? Are we being invaded?'

Still clutching the spoon, Pietro peered over her shoulder. 'It's a helicopter, madam.' His cheerful smile faded and he straightened his chef's whites and looked nervously at Emilio. 'His Royal Highness has returned.'

Chilled by the wind, and battling with a simmering frustration that two weeks of self-imposed absence hadn't cured, Casper sprang from the helicopter and strode towards the house.

Although he'd managed to put several countries and a stretch of water between them, he'd failed to wipe Holly from his thoughts. Even the combined demands of complex state business and the successful conclusion to negotiations guaranteeing billions of dollars of foreign investment hadn't succeeded in pressing the stop button on the non-stop erotic fantasy that had dominated his mind since that day at the rugby.

Even while part of him was angry with her for her ruthless manipulation, another part of his mind was thinking about her incredible legs. He knew she was a liar, but what really stayed in his head was her enticing smile and the taste of her mouth.

And that was fine. Because her manipulation had given him a solution to his problem.

As he approached the house, two uniformed soldiers that he didn't recognise opened the doors for him, backs ramrod straight, eyes forward.

Casper stopped. '*Where* is Emilio?'

One of them cleared his throat. 'I believe he is in the kitchen, Your Highness.'

'The *kitchen*?' Casper approached a nervous footman. 'Since when did my kitchen represent a major security risk?'

'I believe he is with Miss Phillips and the rest of the staff, sir.'

Having personally delivered the order that Emilio should watch her, Casper relaxed a fraction. Contemplating the difficult two weeks Holly must have had with his battle-hardened security chief, he almost smiled. Emilio had been known to drive soldiers to tears, but he felt no sympathy for her. After all, *she* was the one who had decided to name him as the father of her unborn baby. She deserved everything she had coming to her.

Striding towards the kitchen with that thought uppermost in his mind, he pushed open the door, astonished to hear the rare sound of Emilio's laughter, and even more surprised to see his usually reserved Head of Security straighten a clasp in Holly's vibrant curls in an unmistakeably affectionate manner.

Holly was smiling gratefully and Casper felt like an interloper, intruding on a private moment. Experiencing a wild surge of quite inexplicable anger, he stood in the doorway.

The rest of the staff were eating and chatting, and Emilio was the first to notice him. 'Your Highness.' Evidently shocked at seeing the prince in the kitchen, he stiffened respectfully. 'I was just about to come upstairs and meet you.'

'But you had other things to distract you,' Casper observed tightly, strolling into the kitchen and taking in the empty plates and the smell of baking in a single, sweeping glance.

Without waiting for him to issue the order, the various members of his household staff rose to their feet and hastily left the room.

Pietro hesitated and then he, too, melted away without being asked.

Only Emilio didn't move.

Casper slowly undid the buttons on his long coat. 'I'm sure you have many demands on your time, Emilio,' he said softly, but the bodyguard stood still.

'My priority is protecting Miss Phillips, sir.'

'That's true.' Casper removed his coat and dropped it over the back of the nearest chair. 'But not,' he said gently, 'From me.'

Emilio hesitated and glanced at Holly. 'You have the alarm I gave you, madam, should you need me for anything.'

There was no missing the affection in Holly's smile. 'I'll be fine, Emilio, but thank you.'

Watching this interchange with speechless incredulity, Casper was engulfed by a wave of anger so violent that it shook him.

Against his will he was transported back eight years, and suddenly he was seeing another woman smiling at another man.

Pain cut through the red mist of his anger, and he glanced down at his hand and realised that he was gripping the back of the chair so tightly his knuckles were white.

'Your Highness?' Holly's voice penetrated his brain. 'Are you all right?'

Locking down his thoughts with ruthless focus, Casper transferred his gaze to Holly, but the bitter taste of betrayal remained. 'Emilio is a married man. *Do you have no sense of decency?*'

'I—I'm sorry?'

'I've no doubt his wife and child will be sorry, too.'

Her expression changed from concern to anger. 'How dare you? How dare you turn everything beautiful into something sordid. Emilio and I are friends—nothing more.' She lifted a hand to her head. 'Oh God, I can't believe you'd even think— *what is the matter with you?* It's almost as if you believe the worst of people so that you can't be disappointed.'

Was that what he did? Stunned by that accusation, Casper felt as cold as marble. 'Despite a short acquaintance, Emilio would clearly die for you.'

'We've been living in each other's pockets for two weeks— what did you expect? On second thoughts, don't answer that.' She took a deep breath. 'Look, maybe you don't know me well enough to know *I* wouldn't do that, but you know Emilio. He was telling me that he's been with you for twenty years! How could you think that of someone so close to you?'

Because he knew only too well that it was the people closest to you who were capable of the greatest betrayal. And causing the greatest pain.

Casper released his grip on the chair and flexed his bloodless fingers.

'Whatever the nature of your relationship, Emilio is in charge of my security. He can't perform his duties effectively if he's flirting in the kitchen.'

'Nor can he perform his duties on an empty stomach. We were eating lunch, not flirting. Or aren't your staff allowed to eat lunch?'

'You're not a member of my staff.' Casper glanced round the homely kitchen. 'And there is a formal dining-room upstairs for your use.'

'It's as big as a barn, and I don't want to eat on my own. Where's the fun in that?' Her expression made it clear that she thought it should have been obvious that eating alone was a stupid idea. 'Sorry, but sitting alone at one end of a vast table is a bit sad. I prefer the company of real people, not paintings.'

'So you've been distracting Emilio.'

'Actually, yes. I've been trying to take his mind off his worries.' Her shoulders stiffened defensively. 'Did *you* know that his little boy has been taken into hospital? And he's been stuck here with me, fretting himself to death while—'

The anger drained from Casper. 'His son is ill?'

'Yes, and he—'

'What is wrong with the child?'

'Well, it started with a very high temperature. I don't think his wife was too worried at that point, so she gave him the usual stuff but nothing seemed to bring his temperature down. Then she was putting him to bed when—'

'What is wrong with the child?' Impatient for the facts, Casper sliced through her chatter, and she gave him a hurt look.

'I'm *trying* to tell you! You're the one who keeps interrupting.'

Attempting to control his temper, Casper inhaled deeply. 'Summarise.'

'I *was* summarising.' Affronted, she glared at him. 'So, his temperature went up and up and then he had a fit, which apparently can be normal for a toddler because they're hopeless at controlling their temperature, and so they took him in and did some tests and—'

'That isn't a summary, it's a three-act play!' Exasperated, Casper strode across to her and placed a finger over her mouth. 'Stop talking for one minute and answer my question in no more than three words—*what is wrong with Emilio's son?*'

Her lips were soft against his finger and he felt the warmth of her breath as she parted her lips to respond.

'Virus,' she muttered, and Casper withdrew his hand as if he'd been scalded, taken aback by the rush of sexual heat that engulfed him. The urge to take possession of her luscious mouth was so strong that he took a step backwards.

'And is his condition improving?'

'Yes, but—'

'That's all I need to know.' Needing space, Casper turned and strode purposefully towards the door, but she hurtled after him and caught his arm.

'No! No, it isn't all you need to know! "Virus" and "improving" doesn't give you a clue about what it's been like for poor Emilio! Those are just facts, but it's the feelings that matter.' She waved an arm. 'He was stuck here with me while they were doing all these tests, and he was worried sick and—' She broke off, clearly unsettled by his silence. 'Don't you *care*? You're *so* cold! Y-you just stand there looking at me, not saying anything. What do you think it's been like for Emilio being stuck here with me while his little boy is ill?'

Casper scanned her flushed cheeks and lifted an eyebrow in sardonic mockery. 'Noisy?'

Her hand fell from his arm. 'I'm only talking too much because you make me nervous.'

Only both of them knew that there was more than nerves shimmering between them.

It was there in her eyes—awareness, excitement, longing.

Distancing himself, Casper yanked open the door. 'Then I'll give you a moment to collect yourself.' He left the room, issued a set of instructions to a waiting security-guard, and then returned to the kitchen to find Holly pacing the room in agitation.

She threw him a reproachful look. 'All right, maybe I do talk a lot, but that's just the way I am, and nobody's perfect. And you're the one who left me here without even telling me when you'd be back!' Her chin lifted. 'Did you think I'd sit in silence for two weeks?'

Casper strode over to the large table and poured himself a glass of water from the jug on the table. 'It was fairly obvious to me from our last meeting that you and silence have never been intimately acquainted.'

'Well, I don't expect you to understand, because you're obviously the strong silent type who uses words like each one costs a fortune, but I like people. I like talking to them.'

And they liked talking to her, if the buzz of conversation around the kitchen table had been anything to go by.

And she knew about Emilio's son.

Casper tried to remember a time when people had been that open with him, and realised that they never had been.

Even before tragedy had befallen the royal family of Santallia, he'd lived a life of privileged isolation. Because of his position, people were rarely open and honest.

And he'd learned the hard way that trust was one gift he couldn't afford to bestow.

Because of his error of judgement, his country had suffered.

And now he had the chance to make amends. *To give the people what they wanted.*

And as for the rest of it—physically the chemistry between them was explosive, and that was all he required.

He drank deeply and then put the glass down, his eyes locking with hers.

Immediately engulfed by a dangerous tension, Casper tried to analyse what it was about her that he found so irresistibly sexy.

Not her dress sense, that was for sure. Her ancient jeans had a rip in the knees, her pale-pink jumper was obviously an old favourite, and the colour in her cheeks had more to do with the heat coming from the Aga than artful use of make-up.

Accustomed to women who groomed themselves to within an inch of their lives, he found her lack of artifice oddly refreshing.

Her beauty wasn't the result of expensive cosmetics or the hand of a skilled surgeon. Holly was vibrant, passionate and desperately sexy, and all he wanted to do was flatten her to the table and re-enact every sizzling moment of their first meeting.

Exasperated and baffled by the strength of that inappropriate urge, Casper dragged his eyes back to her face. 'Emilio failed to pass on the message that you were to buy a new wardrobe.'

'No. He told me.' She hooked her thumbs into the waistband of her jeans and the movement revealed a tantalising glimpse of smooth, flat stomach. 'I just didn't need anything. What do I need a new wardrobe for? I've spent the mornings helping Ivy and the afternoons helping Jim prune the trees in the orchard.'

'*Who* is Ivy?'

'Your housekeeper. She lost her husband eight months ago and she's been very down, but she has started joining us for lunch, and she's been talking about— Sorry.' She raised a hand in wary apology. 'I forgot you just want facts. OK, facts. I can do that. Ivy. Housekeeper. Depressed. Improving.' She ticked them off her fingers. 'How's that? You're smiling, so I must have done OK.'

Surprised to discover that he was indeed smiling, Casper shook his head slowly. 'Your gift for conversation has clearly given you a great deal of information about my staff.'

'It's important to understand people you work with.'

'When I left you here, my intention was not for you to work alongside the staff.'

'I had to do something with my day. You gave orders that I couldn't leave the premises. I was trapped here.'

'You were brought here for your own safety.'

'Was I?' Her brilliant green eyes glowed bright with scepticism. 'Or was I brought here for *your* safety, so that I couldn't talk to the press?'

'That particular boat has already sailed,' Casper said tightly, his temper flaring at her untimely reminder of just how effectively she'd manipulated the media. 'You're here for your protection.'

'Do you have any idea how weird that sounds?' Holly glanced pointedly at the rip in her jeans. 'I mean, one minute I'm a waitress who no one notices unless they want to complain about their food, and the next I'm someone who needs twenty-four-hour protection.'

'You're carrying the heir to the throne.'

'And that's all that matters?' She tilted her head to one side, studying his expression. 'You'll put aside your personal feelings for me because of the baby?'

What personal feelings?

Emotion had no place in his life.

On one previous occasion he'd allowed himself to be ruled by emotion and the consequences had been devastating.

As far as he was concerned, his relationship with Holly was a business transaction, nothing more.

Casper stared into her anxious green eyes, wondering why she didn't look more triumphant.

She'd successfully secured a future for herself and her child.

Or was she suddenly realising just how high a price she'd paid for that particular social leap?

'I don't want to discuss this again.' Crushing any future urge on her part to dwell on the unfortunate circumstances of their wedding, Casper strolled forward, realising that he hadn't yet revealed the reason for his return.

'Y—you're a bit crabby. Perhaps you need to eat,' she said helpfully, scooping up a plate from the table. 'Try one of Pietro's pastries. It's a new recipe and they're really delicious.'

'I'm not hungry.' His intention had just been to deliver his orders and then spend the afternoon catching up on official papers. He hadn't expected to be drawn into a discussion.

Nor had he expected an ongoing battle with his libido.

'Just taste them.' Apparently unaware of his reluctance, she broke off a piece of the pastry and lifted it to his lips. 'They're fresh out of the oven. Try.'

Drowning in her subtle floral scent and her smile, Casper's senses reeled and he grasped for control. 'I have things to tell you.'

'Eat first.'

Casper ate the pastry and wished he hadn't, because as his lips touched her fingers again he was immediately plunged into an erotic, sensual world that featured Holly as the leading lady in a scene dominated by scented oils and silk sheets.

She withdrew her hand slowly, her eyes darkening as they both silently acknowledged the dangerous sexual charge that suffused every communication they shared.

'What is it you need to tell me, Your Highness?'

'Casper.'

For the space of a heartbeat, she looked at him and then she gave a twisted smile. 'I don't think so. I'm not comfortable enough with you. Maybe it's just because you've had a long journey, but you're very cold. Intimidating. I feel as though you're going to say "off with her head" any minute.'

'You can't call me Your Highness in the wedding ceremony.'

Shock flared in her eyes. 'I sort of assumed the wedding was off. You haven't *once* phoned me whilst you've been away.'

Casper thought of the number of times he'd reached for the phone before he'd realised what he was doing. 'I had nothing to say.'

Holly lifted her hands and made a sound that was somewhere between a sob and laughter. 'Well, if you had nothing to say to me in two weeks, it doesn't bode well for a lifetime together, does it? But I do have things I want to say to you.' She drew in a breath. 'Starting with your offer of marriage. I've given it a lot of thought.'

'That doesn't surprise me. I expect it's been two weeks of non-stop self-congratulation while you enjoy your new life and reflect on the future.' His cynical observation was met with appalled silence and she stared at him for a moment, her delicate features suddenly pinched and white.

Then the plate slipped from her hands and smashed on the kitchen floor, scattering china and pastry everywhere.

'How *dare* you say that? You have a real gift for saying really horrible things.' Her small hands curled into fists by her sides. *'Have you any idea how hard all of this is for me?* Well, let me tell you what my life has been like since you walked into it!

'First there is that huge picture of me on the screen so the whole world can see the size of my bottom, then the press crawl all over my life, exposing things about me that I haven't even told my closest friends and making me out to be some psycho nutcase. *Then* I discover I'm pregnant, and I was really happy about that until you showed up and told me that you didn't believe it was yours. So basically since I've met you I've been portrayed publicly as a fat, abandoned slut with no morals! How's my new life sounding so far, Your Highness? Not good—so don't *talk* to me about how I must be congratulating myself because, believe me, my confidence is at an all-time low.' Her breathing rapid, she sucked in several breaths and Casper, who detested emotional scenes, erected barriers faster than a bank being robbed.

'I warned you that—'

'I haven't finished!' She glared at him. 'You think this is an easy decision for me, but it isn't! This is our baby's future we're talking about! And, whatever you may think, I didn't plan this. Which is why I've done nothing but agonise over what to do for the past two weeks. *Obviously* I don't want to be married to a man who can't stand the sight of me, but neither do I want my baby to be without a father. It's been a horrible, *horrible* choice, and frankly I wouldn't wish it on anyone! And if you need that summarised in two words I'd pick "scary" and "sacrifice".'

In the process of formulating an exit strategy, Casper looked at her with raw incredulity. '*Sacrifice*?'

'Yes. Because, although I'm sure having a father is right for our baby, I'm *not* sure that being married to you is right for me. And there's no need to use that tone. I don't care about the prince bit, nor do I care about your castle or your bank account.' Her voice was hoarse. 'But I won't have our child growing up thinking that his father abandoned him. And that's why I'll marry you. By the time he's old enough to understand what is going on, you will have realised how wrong you are about me and given me a big, fat apology. But don't think this is easy for me. I have no wish to marry a man who can't talk about his feelings and doesn't show affection.'

Casper responded to this last declaration with genuine astonishment. 'Affection?' How could she possibly think he'd feel affection for a woman who had good as slapped him with a paternity suit?

She rolled her eyes. 'You see? Even the word makes you nervous, and that says everything, doesn't it? You were quite happy to have hot sex with me, but anything else is completely alien to you.' She covered her face with her hands, and her voice choked. 'Oh, what am I doing? How can we even *think* about getting married when there's nothing between us?'

'We share a very powerful sexual chemistry, or we wouldn't be in this position right now,' Casper responded instantly, and her hands dropped and she gave a disbelieving laugh.

'Well, that's romantic. There's no mistaking your priorities. Summarised in three words, it would be sex, sex, sex.'

'Don't underestimate the importance of sex,' Casper breathed, watching as her lips parted slightly. 'If we're going to be sharing a bed night after night, it helps that I find you attractive.' Surprisingly, his statement appeared to finally silence her.

She stared at him, her eyes wide, her lips slightly parted. Then she rubbed her hands over her jeans in a self-conscious gesture. 'You find me—attractive? Really?'

'*Obviously* your dress sense needs considerable work,' he said silkily. 'And generally speaking I'm not wild about jeans, although I have to confess that you manage to look good in them. Apart from that, and as long as you don't *ever* wear anything featuring a cartoon once you're officially sleeping in my bed, yes, I'll find you attractive.'

A laugh burst from her throat. 'I can't believe you're telling me how to dress—or that I'm listening.'

'I'm not telling you how to dress. I'm telling you how to keep me interested. It's up to you whether you follow the advice or not.'

'And that's supposed to be enough? A marriage based on sex?' She shook her head slowly. 'It doesn't make sense. I still don't understand why, if you genuinely don't believe this is your baby, you'd be willing to marry me. Instead of facts, why don't you give me feelings?'

He didn't have feelings.

He hadn't allowed himself feelings for eight years.

'Given all the research you did on the royal house of Santallia, I would think you'd be aware of the reasons. I'm the last of the line. I'm expected to produce an heir. To the outside world, it appears that I've done that.'

'You're giving me facts again,' she said softly. 'How do you *feel*, Your Highness?'

Ignoring her question, Casper paced over to the window, his tension levels soaring. 'The people of Santallia are currently in a state of celebration. The moment the story broke on the news, they were making plans for the royal wedding. There will be fireworks and state banquets. Apparently my popularity rating has soared. School children have already been queuing outside the palace with home-made cards and teddies for the baby—little girls with stars in their eyes.' He turned, looking for signs of remorse. 'Are you feeling guilty yet, Holly? Is your conscience pricking you?'

'Teddies?' Instead of retreating in the face of his harsh words, she appeared visibly moved by the picture he'd painted. Her hand slid to her stomach in an instinctively protective gesture, and he saw tears of emotion glisten in her eyes. 'They're that pleased? It *is* wonderful that everyone is longing for you to get married and have a baby. You must be very touched that they care so much.'

'It's because they care so much that we're standing here now.'

Her gaze held his. 'So, if they wanted you to have a baby so badly, and you're so keen to please them, why haven't you done it before? Why haven't you married and given them an heir?' She broke off abruptly and he knew from the guilty flush on her cheeks that her research had included details about his past relationships.

He could almost see her mind working, thinking that she knew what was going on in his.

Fortunately, she didn't have a clue.

No one did. He'd made sure of that.

The truth was safely buried where it could do no harm. *And it was going to stay buried.*

Observing his lack of response, she sighed. 'What's going on in your head? I don't understand you!'

'I don't require you to understand me,' Casper said in a cool tone. 'I just require you to play the part you auditioned for. From now on, you'll just do as you're told. You'll smile when I tell you to smile and you'll walk where I tell you to walk. In return, you'll have more money than you know how to spend, and a lifestyle that most of the world will envy.'

She opened her mouth and closed it again, her face a mask of indecision. 'I don't know. I really don't know.' She stooped and started picking up pieces of broken china, as if she needed to do something with her hands. 'I thought I'd made up my mind, but now I'm not sure. How can I accept your proposal when you *scare* me? You use three words, I use thirty. I've never met anyone so emotionally detached. I—I'm just not comfortable with you.' She put the china carefully on the table.

'Comfortable?'

She rubbed her fingers over her forehead, as if her brain was aching and she wanted to soothe it. 'We'll hardly be great parents if I'm bracing myself for conflict every time you enter a room. And then there's the fact that I don't exactly fit the profile of perfect princess.'

'The only thing that matters is that the world thinks you're carrying my child. As far as the people of Santallia are concerned, that makes you the perfect princess.'

'But not *your* perfect princess. You don't seem to care who you marry. Did you love her very much?' She blurted out the question as though she couldn't stop herself, and then gave an apologetic sigh. 'I'm sorry. Perhaps I shouldn't. But you lost your fiancée, Antonia, and it's stupid to pretend that I don't know about it, because everyone knew—'

No one knew.

'Enough!' Stunned that she would dare tread on such dangerous territory, Casper sent her a warning glance, and in that single unsettling moment he had the feeling that she was looking deep inside him.

'I *am* sorry,' she said quietly. 'Because I certainly don't want to hurt you. But I don't see how we're going to have any sort of marriage when you won't let another human being get close. You create this barrier around you. Frankly, how I ever felt relaxed enough with you to have sex, I have no idea. At the moment my insides feel as though I swallowed a knotted rope.' But even as she said the words the tension in the air crackled and snapped, and he saw her chest rise and fall as her breathing quickened.

The sexual chemistry was more powerful than both of them, and Casper wasn't even aware that he'd moved until his hands slid into her hair and he felt her lips parting in response to the explicit demands of his mouth.

Enforced abstinence and sexual denial had simply increased the feverish craving, and he hauled her hard against him, driven by a sensual urgency previously unknown to him.

Her lips were soft and sweet, and the scent and taste of her closed over him, drowning his senses until every rational thought was blown from his brain by a powerful rush of erotic pleasure.

She moaned with desperation, her arms winding round his neck, her body trembling against his as she arched in sensual invitation, her abandoned response a blatant invitation to further intimacy.

In the grip of an almost agonising arousal, Casper closed possessive hands over her hips and lifted her onto the kitchen table. She was pliant and shivering against him, the sensuous movements of her body shamelessly urging him on.

And then the gentle hiss of water boiling on the Aga penetrated the red fog in his mind and he froze, his seeking hands suddenly still as he realised what he was doing.

And where he was doing it.

Another time, another table.

Deploring the lack of control that gripped him whenever he was with this woman, he dragged his mouth from hers with a huge effort of will, and stared down into her dazed, shocked eyes. Her mouth was damp and swollen from his kiss, and she was shaking with the same wild excitement that was driving him.

His usual self-restraint severely challenged by her addictive sexuality, Casper released his grip on her hips and stepped backwards.

'Hopefully that should have satisfied any worries you might have about whether or not you'll be able to relax with me when the time comes.'

She slid off the table, her fingers fastened tightly round the edge for support. 'Your Highness.' Her voice was smoky with passion. 'Casper—'

'We're short on time.' Ruthlessly withdrawing from the softness he saw in her eyes, he glanced at his watch. 'I've flown in a team of people to help you prepare.'

'Prepare for what?' Her eyes dropped to his mouth, and it was obvious that she wasn't really listening to what he was saying—*that her body was still struggling with the electricity that sparked between them.*

'The wedding. We fly to Santallia tonight. We're getting married tomorrow.' He paused, allowing time for his words to sink in. 'And that's not a proposal, Holly. It's an order.'

CHAPTER FIVE

THE roar of the crowd reached deafening proportions, and the long avenue leading from the cathedral to the palace was a sea of smiling faces and waving flags.

'I can't believe the number of people,' Holly said faintly as she settled herself in the golden carriage. The rings on the third finger of her left hand felt heavy and unfamiliar, and she glanced down in disbelief. 'And I can't believe we're married. You certainly don't hang around, do you? You could have given me a little more warning.'

'Why?'

Why? Only Casper could ask that question, she thought wryly. Fiddling nervously with the enormous diamond ring, she wondered whether there was something wrong with her. Here she was, living a life straight out of the pages of a child's fairy tale, and she would have swapped the lot for some kind words from the man next to her.

Her life was moving ahead too fast for comfort.

Having spent the previous afternoon with a top dress designer who had apparently cleared her schedule to accommodate the prince's request to dress his bride, she'd been transferred by helicopter to the royal flight and then arrived in the Mediterranean principality of Santallia as the sun was setting.

'I loved The Dowager Cottage, by the way.'

'It was built for my great-great grandmother so that she could escape occasionally from the formality of life in the palace. I'm pleased you were comfortable.'

Physically, yes, but mentally…

Unable to sleep, Holly had spent most of the night sitting on the balcony that looked over the sea, thinking about what was to come.

Thinking about Casper.

Hoping she was doing the right thing.

Exhausted from thinking and worrying, she'd eventually sprawled on the bed, only to be woken by an army of dress designers, hairdressers and make-up artists prepared to turn her from gauche waitress into princess. And then she'd been driven through this same cheering crowd to the cathedral that dominated the main square of Santallia Town.

She remembered very little of the actual service—very little except the memory of Casper standing powerful and confident by her side as they exchanged vows. And at that moment she'd been filled with a conviction that she was doing the right thing.

She was giving her baby a father. A stability that she'd never had. *Roots and a family.*

How could that be a mistake?

As the carriage began to move forward down the tree-lined avenue, she glanced at the prince, only to find him studying her intently.

Startlingly handsome in his military uniform, Casper lifted her hand to his lips in an old-fashioned gesture that was greeted with cheers of approval from the crowd. 'The dress is a great improvement on ripped jeans,' he drawled, and she glanced down at herself, fingering the embroidered silk with reverential fingers.

'It's impressive what a top designer can do when required,

although I was terrified of tripping over on those steps.' She couldn't take her eyes from the cheering crowd. Everywhere she looked there were smiling faces and waving flags. 'They *really* love you.'

'They're here to see you, not me,' he said dryly, but she remembered what she'd read about him on the Internet—about his devotion to his country—and knew it wasn't true.

Although he'd never expected to rule, Prince Casper had stepped into the role, burying his own personal grief in order to bring stability to a country in turmoil.

And they loved him for it.

'Do you ever wish you weren't the prince?' The question left her lips before she could stop it and he gave a faint smile.

'You have a real gift for voicing questions that other people keep as thoughts.' He relaxed in the seat, undaunted by the crowds of well-wishers. 'And the answer is no, I don't wish it. I love my country.'

He loved his country so much that he'd marry a woman he didn't love because the people expected it.

Holly glanced at the sun-baked pavements and then at the perfect blue sky. 'It's beautiful here,' she agreed. 'When I looked out of the window this morning, the first thing I saw was the sea. It felt like being on holiday.'

'You looked very pale during the service.' His eyes lingered on her face. 'You were on your feet for a long time. I was worried that you might keel over.'

'And presumably a prostrate bride wouldn't have done anything for your public image,' she said lightly. 'I was fine.'

'I'm reliably informed that the early weeks of pregnancy are often the most exhausting.'

He'd talked to someone about her pregnancy? Her heart lurched, and it suddenly occurred to her just how little she knew about his life here. Had he been talking to a woman?

She was aware that his name had been linked with a number of European beauties. Was he…?

'No,' he drawled. 'I wasn't.'

Her eyes widened. 'I didn't say anything—'

'But you were thinking it,' he said dryly. 'And the answer is no, my conversation wasn't with a lover. It was with a doctor.'

'Oh.' She blushed scarlet, mortified that her thoughts had been so transparent, but filled with unimaginable relief that he hadn't asked another woman. 'When did you speak to a doctor?'

'While you were at Foxcourt Manor, I interviewed a handful of the top European obstetricians. It's important that you feel comfortable with your doctor. After all, you're not good with detached and cold, are you?' He gave a faint smile as he alluded to their previous conversation, and Holly was so touched that for a moment she forgot the presence of the cheering, waving crowd.

'You did that for me?'

'I don't want you upset.'

'That was incredibly thoughtful.' She wanted to ask whether he'd really done it for her or the baby, but decided that it didn't matter. The fact that he'd noticed that much about her personality was encouraging.

'You're stunning,' he murmured, his gaze lingering on her glossy mouth and dropping to the demure neckline of her dress. 'The perfect bride. And you've coped with the crowd really well. I'm proud of you.'

'Really?' Deciding not to mention the fact that she found *him* far more intimidating than any crowd, Holly relaxed for the first time in what felt like an eternity. She felt drugged by happiness and weak with relief at the change in him.

He was unusually attentive and much more approachable.

Perhaps, she mused silently, he'd finally deduced that the baby must be his.

What other explanation was there for his sudden change of attitude?

'And now you need to fulfil your first duty as royal princess.' He smiled down at her. 'Smile and wave at the crowd. They're expecting it.'

Finding it hard to believe that anyone would care whether she waved at them or not, Holly tentatively raised her hand, and the immediate roar of approval from the crowd made her blink in amazement. 'But I'm just someone ordinary,' she muttered, and the prince's eyes gleamed with wry amusement.

'That's why they love you. You're living proof that fairy-tale endings can happen to ordinary people.'

The last of her insecurities faded and Holly gave a bubble of laughter, her mood lifting still further as she saw the smiles of genuine delight on the faces of the people pressing against the barriers.

Flanked by mounted guards, the carriage moved slowly down the tree-lined avenue, and ahead of her she was surprised to see Emilio's bulky frame.

'But you sent Emilio home.' Puzzled, she glanced at the prince. 'He came to say goodbye to me yesterday, and told me that you'd been brilliant.'

'He insisted on returning this morning.' Casper gave a faint smile. 'On such a huge public occasion he refused to entrust your security to anyone else.'

'Oh, that's so kind.' Incredibly touched, Holly gave Emilio a wave. 'There do seem to be millions of people. What's this street like on a normal day?'

Casper settled back against the seat. 'The road leads directly to the palace. It's a favourite tourist route. Turn to the right at the bottom, and you reach the sea.'

Holly was still smiling at the crowd when she saw a toddler stumble and fall to the ground, his little body trapped against the metal barriers by the sheer pressure of the crowd. 'Oh no!

Stop the coach!' Before Casper could respond, Holly opened
the door of the carriage, hitched her white silk dress up round
her middle and jumped down into the road.

Oblivious to the havoc she was creating in the security operation, she hurried across to the bawling toddler and the
panicking mum. 'Is he all right? Oh my goodness—can
everyone move back a bit, please?' Raising her voice and ges-
turing at the crowd, she breathed a sigh of relief as everyone
shifted slightly and she saw the mother safely lift the sobbing
child. 'Phew. It's a bit crowded, isn't it? Is he all right? There—
don't cry, sweetheart. Have you got a smile for me?' She
reached out to the child who immediately stopped crying and
stared at her in wonder.

'It's your tiara, Your Royal Highness, it's all sparkly, and
he loves everything sparkly.' The woman flushed scarlet. 'We
all wanted to get a good view of you, madam.'

Holly noticed a trickle of blood on the child's forehead.
'He's cut his head on the barrier. Does someone have a plaster?'

'Holly.'

Hearing her name, she looked over her shoulder and saw
Casper striding towards her, a strange expression on his face.
'Holly, you're giving the security team heart-failure.'

'I'm sorry about that, but do you have a handkerchief or
something?' She glanced anxiously back at the toddler who
now had his thumb in his mouth.

Casper hesitated and then produced a handkerchief from
the pocket of his uniform.

Holly took it and leaned over the barrier to press it gently
against the toddler's forehead. 'There. It doesn't look too bad
when you look at it closely.' One of the security team
produced a plaster and vaulted the barrier to deal with the
child, and Holly suddenly realised that the crowd was
cheering for Casper.

The prince delivered a charismatic smile and slipped his arm round his bride. 'Next time, don't leave the coach. It isn't safe.'

'It isn't safe for that toddler, either. People are crushing too close to the barriers. What was I supposed to do?' She knew it was foolish to read too much into his comment, but she couldn't help it. Would he warn her not to leave the coach if he didn't care about her?

The cheering intensified, and then there was a yell from the crowd that turned into a chant.

'Kiss her, Prince Casper! *Kiss, kiss, kiss…!*'

Holly blushed scarlet but Casper, clearly as experienced at seducing a crowd as he was women, pulled her gently into his arms and lowered his mouth to hers with his usual cool confidence. Stunned by the unexpected gentleness of that kiss, Holly melted against him, stars exploding in her head and her heart.

Would he kiss her like that if he didn't care?

Surely it was another sign that he finally believed that she must be telling the truth? *That he'd been wrong about her.*

The crowd gave a collective sigh of approval, and when Casper finally lifted his head there was another enormous roar of approval.

'Now you've charmed the crowd, we need to go back to the coach.' Amusement in his eyes, he tucked her hand into his arm. 'And you need to stop jumping out of carriages and behave with some decorum. Not only are you now a princess, but you're a pregnant princess.'

'I know, but—' She glanced towards the crowd. 'Some of these people have been standing outside all night, even the children—do we have to go in the carriage? Couldn't we just walk? We could chat to people along the way.'

Casper's dark brows locked in a disapproving frown. 'It would be a major security risk.'

'I *know* you don't care about that. When you're in public you always walk. I read that you have a constant argument with your bodyguards and the security services.' She bit her lip, suddenly wishing she hadn't reminded him of her Internet moment, but he simply smiled and took her hand firmly in his.

'In this instance I was thinking of *your* safety. Don't you find the crowds daunting?'

'I think it's lovely that they've made the effort to come and see me get married,' Holly confessed. Spying two small girls holding a bunch of flowers that they obviously picked themselves, she pushed her elaborate bouquet towards an astonished Casper and hurried across. 'Are those for me? They're so pretty. Are they from your garden?' She talked to the girls, then to their mother, shook what felt like a million hands, and slowly and gradually made her way along the avenue towards the palace. But it took a long time because everyone had something to say to her and she had plenty to say in return.

Several people pushed teddies into her arms for the baby, and eventually she needed help to carry everything.

After an hour of chatting to a stunned and delighted crowd, Holly finally allowed herself to be urged back into the carriage.

'Clearly I misjudged you.' Casper settled himself beside her, indicating with his head that the procession should move on.

Holly's heart soared. 'Y-you did?'

'Yes. I thought you'd find the whole day impossibly daunting. But you're a natural.' He gave a wry smile. 'I've never seen anyone so skilled at talking about nothing with such enthusiasm and for such a long time.'

Holly digested this statement, decided that it was a compliment of sorts, and tried not to be disappointed that he'd been referring to the way she'd handled herself in public, rather than his opinion of her pregnancy.

Reminding herself that she had to be patient, she smiled. 'How can it be daunting when everyone is so nice?' Holly waved again and spied another group of children in the crowd. She opened her mouth to ask if they could stop, but Casper met her questioning glance with a slow shake of his head.

'No. Absolutely not. Delighted though I am that you've managed to please the crowd, we have about two-hundred foreign dignitaries and heads of state currently waiting for us at the palace and we're already late. I'd rather not cause a diplomatic incident if we can avoid it.' But his tone was in direct contrast to the warmth in his eyes. 'You've done well, *tesoro*.'

His praise made her glow inside and out, and she felt so ridiculously happy that she couldn't stop smiling. All right, so they'd had a shaky start to their relationship, but one of the advantages of that was that it could only improve.

Feeling optimistic about the future, Holly smiled all the way through the formal banquet, all the way through the dancing and all the way up to the moment when she was finally escorted to the prince's private quarters in a wing of the palace suspended above the sea.

It was only as the door closed behind them, leaving the guests and the guards on the outside, that reality hit her.

They were alone.

And this was their wedding night.

Gripped by a sudden attack of nerves, Holly gave a faltering smile, instinctively breaking the throbbing, tense silence that had descended on them. 'So this is where you actually live. It's beautiful—so much light and space, and—'

'*Stop* talking.' Casper reached for her clenched hands, gently prised them apart and then slid them round his waist and backed her against the door with an unmistakeable sense of purpose.

Trapped between solid oak and six foot two of raw male

virility, Holly found she could barely breathe, let alone talk. Dry mouthed, knees shaking, she was aware only of the simmering undercurrents of sexuality that emanated from his powerful frame as he took her face in strong, determined hands, his mouth on a direct collision course with hers.

Holly closed her eyes in willing surrender, senses singing, nerves on fire. When the kiss didn't come, she whimpered a faint protest. 'Casper?'

His mouth hovered a breath from hers. 'Open your eyes.'

Her eyes opened obediently and she stared up at him, her heart skipping several beats as she scanned the aristocratic lines of his masculine features. 'Please—kiss me.'

'I intend to do a great deal more than that, *angelo mio...*'

Held captive by his lazy, confident gaze her heart started to pound, and searing heat pooled low in her pelvis. She probably should have played it cool, but Holly was too aroused to remember the meaning of cool.

Her body was in the grip of a strong, explosive excitement that simply intensified as his mouth finally glided onto hers with effortless skill.

His tongue probed the interior of her mouth with erotic expertise, and Holly just melted, moaning low in her throat as his strong hands brought her writhing hips into contact with his potent masculine arousal.

'Not here.' His voice thickened, he pulled away from her and scooped her easily into his arms. 'This time, *tesoro*, we'll make it to the bed. And we're taking our time over it.' He strode through several rooms and then up a winding staircase that led to a bedroom in a turret.

Trembling, *mortified* by how much she wanted him, Holly clutched at his shoulders as he set her down on the floor, barely conscious of the beautiful circular room, the high arched windows or the vaulted ceiling. Her body was on fire with anticipation, and her entire focus was on the man now undressing her with deft, experienced fingers.

As tens of thousands of pounds worth of designer silk slithered unrestrained to the floor, her old insecurities resurfaced, and Holly was grateful for the relative protection of moonlight and underwear. But Casper showed merciless disregard for her inhibitions, peeling off her panties in a slick, decisive movement and tumbling her trembling, naked body onto the enormous four-poster bed.

'Don't move. I like looking at you.' Having positioned her to his satisfaction, Casper sprang to his feet and removed his own clothing with impatient fingers, his eyes scanning her squirming body and flushed cheeks as he undressed with unself-conscious grace and fluidity. 'You are *so* beautiful.'

As his carelessly discarded clothes hit the floor, Holly quickly discovered that there was more than enough light for her to make out bronzed skin and bold male arousal. Dizzy from that brief glimpse of raw masculinity, she drew in a sharp breath as he came down on top of her.

Shocked by the sudden contact with his lean, powerful frame, Holly's pulse rate shot into overdrive and she slid her hands over his shoulders, her back arching as his clever mouth fastened over her nipple, and he plundered her sensitive flesh with sure, skilled flicks of his tongue.

Lightning bursts of sensation exploded through her body, and as his seeking fingers traced a path to that place where the ache had become almost intolerable Holly shifted restlessly against the silk sheets, the wanton movement giving him the access he needed.

With slow, sensitive strokes, he explored the most intimate part of her until Holly was sobbing his name, begging him for more, in the grip of such a terrifying craving that she knew if he stopped now she'd die.

Casper shifted her hips and his own position, giving her just time to register the silken throb of his arousal before he plunged deep into her moist, aching interior, and her world exploded.

Rocketing from earth to ecstasy, Holly shot straight into a shattering climax, only dimly registering Casper's disbelieving curse and the sudden faltering of his rhythm as his own control was threatened by her body's violent response. Sobbing his name, Holly dug her fingers into the slick flesh of his shoulders, so out of her mind with excitement that she was incapable of doing anything except hold on as each driving thrust drove her back towards paradise.

Her body splintered into pieces again, and this time she felt him reach his own release, and she hugged him tightly, overwhelmed by what had to be the most incredible experience of her life.

'You're a miracle in bed,' Casper said huskily, rolling onto his back and taking her with him.

Stunned by the whole experience, and prepared to snuggle against his chest, Holly gave a whimper of shock as he closed his hands over her hips and lifted her so that she straddled him.

'Casper, we can't!'

But they did.

Again and again, until Holly couldn't think or move.

Finally she lay there, sated and exhausted, one arm draped over his powerful chest, her cheek against the warmth of his bronzed shoulder.

She could hear the sounds of the sea through one of the open windows and she closed her eyes, feeling a rush of happiness.

She no longer had any doubts that she'd done the right thing.

They'd been married for less than a day and already his attitude to her was softening. Yes, he found it hard to talk about his emotions, but he didn't have trouble showing them, did he?

He'd been tender, passionate, demanding, skilled, thoughtful.

Just thinking about it made her body burn again, and she slid her fingers through the dark hairs that hazed his chest, fascinated by the contrast between his body and hers.

'I had no idea it was possible to feel like that.' She spoke softly and gently, and pressed an affectionate kiss against his warm flesh, hugging him tightly. 'You're fantastic—' She broke off as he withdrew from her and sprang from the bed.

Without uttering a single word in response to her unguarded declaration, he strode through a door and slammed it behind him.

Holly flinched at the finality of that sound, and her head filled with a totally unreasonable panic.

He'd left. He'd just walked out without saying anything. Desperate to stop him leaving, she kicked back the tangle of silken covers and sprinted towards the door.

And then she heard the sounds of a shower running and realised that the door led to a bathroom.

A tidal wave of relief surged over her and she stopped. Her limbs suddenly drained of strength, she plopped back onto the bed.

He hadn't walked out.

He wasn't her father.

This was different.

Or was it?

Feeling unsettled, confused and desperately hurt, she lay on her back, staring up at the canopy of the four-poster bed.

Rejection wasn't new to her, was it?

So why did it hurt so badly?

Eventually the noise of the shower stopped and moments later Casper strolled back into the bedroom. He'd pulled on a black robe and his hair was still damp from the shower.

Without looking at her, he walked into what she presumed was a dressing room and emerged wearing a pair of trousers, a fresh shirt in his hand.

'Aren't you coming back to bed? Did I say something?' Feeling intensely vulnerable, Holly sat up in the bed and twisted the ends of her hair with nervous fingers. 'One minute we were lying there having a cuddle and the next you sprang out of bed and stalked off. I feel as though you're upset, but I don't know why.'

'Go to sleep.' He shrugged his shoulders into the shirt and fastened the buttons with strong, sure fingers. *Those same fingers that had driven her wild.*

'How can I possibly sleep? *Talk* to me!' Suddenly it felt wrong to be naked, and she reached for the silk nightdress that someone had laid next to her pillow and pulled it over her head. 'What's wrong? Is it the whole wedding thing?' She wanted to ask whether he was thinking about the fiancée he should have married, Antonia, but she didn't want to risk making the situation worse.

'Go back to bed, Holly.'

'How can I possibly do that? Don't shut me out, Casper.' Her voice cracked and she slid out of bed and walked over to him. 'I'm your *wife*.'

'Precisely.' He looked at her then, and his eyes were cold as ice. 'I have already fulfilled my side of the deal by marrying you.'

Holly froze with shock. 'Deal?'

'You wanted a father for your baby. I needed an heir.'

Her legs buckled and she sank down onto the edge of the bed. 'You make it sound as though I picked you at random.'

'Not at random. I think you targeted me very carefully.'

'You still believe this isn't your baby. Oh God. I really thought you'd changed your mind about that—you seemed different today—and when we—' She glanced at the rumpled sheets on the bed, her eyes glistening with tears. 'You made love to me and it felt—'

'We had sex, Holly.' His voice was devoid of emotion. 'Love didn't come into it, and it never will, make no mistake about that. Don't do that female thing of turning a physical act into something emotional.'

Her hopes exploded like a balloon landing on nails.

'It wasn't just the sex,' she whispered. 'You've been different today. Caring. Ever since the moment I arrived at the cathedral.' Her voice cracked. 'You've been smiling at me, you had your arm around me. *You kissed me.*'

'We're supposed to look as though we're in love.' Apparently unaffected by her mounting distress, he strode over to an antique table next to the window. 'Do you want a drink?'

'No. I don't want a drink!' Her heart was suddenly bumping hard and she felt physically sick. 'Are you saying that everything that happened today was for the benefit of the crowd?'

He poured himself a whisky but didn't touch it. Instead he stared out of the window, his knuckles white on the glass, his handsome face revealing nothing of his thoughts. No emotion. 'They wanted the fairy tale. We gave it to them. That's what we royals have to do. We give the people what they want. In this case, a love match, a wedding and an heir.'

She blinked rapidly, determined to hold back the tears. 'So why did you marry *me*?'

He lifted the glass to his lips. 'Why not?'

'Because you could have married someone you loved.'

He lowered the glass without drinking. 'I don't want love.'

Because he'd had it once and now it was gone?

Holly's throat closed. 'That's a terrible thing to say and a terrible way to feel,' she whispered. 'I know you lost and I know you must have suffered, but—'

'You don't know anything.'

'Then tell me!' She was crying openly now, tears flooding her cheeks. 'I'm devastated that the whole of today was a sham. I know it's difficult for you to talk about Antonia, and frankly it isn't that easy to hear it, either. But I know we're not going to have any sort of marriage unless we're honest with each other.'

Please don't let him walk out on me. Please don't let that happen.

'Honest?' He slammed the glass down onto the table and turned to look at her. 'You lie about your baby, you lie all the way to the altar wearing your symbolic white dress, and then you suggest we're *honest*? It's a little late for that, don't you think?'

'*It's your baby,*' Holly said hoarsely. Her insides were twisted in pain as she felt her new life crumbling around her. 'And I don't know how you can believe otherwise.'

'Don't you? Then let me tell you.' He strolled towards her, his eyes glittering dark and deadly. 'It can't be my baby, Holly, because I can't have children. I don't know whose baby you're carrying, my sweet wife, but I know for sure it isn't mine. I'm infertile.'

CHAPTER SIX

'No.' HOLLY sat down hard on the nearest chair, her heart pounding. 'That isn't possible,' she said hoarsely. 'I am living proof that it isn't possible. Why would you even think that?'

'Eight years ago I had an accident.'

The accident that had killed his brother and Antonia. 'I know about the accident.'

'You know only what I chose to reveal.' He paced across the room and stared out over the ocean. 'Everyone knew that Santallia lost the heir to the throne. Everyone knew my fiancée died. No one knew that the accident crushed my pelvis so badly that my chances of ever fathering a child were nil.'

Holly's mind was in turmoil. 'Casper—'

'We had a crisis on our hands.' He thrust his hands into his pockets, the movement emphasising the hard masculine lines of his body. 'My brother was dead. I was suddenly the ruling prince and I was in intensive care, hitched up to a ventilator. When I recovered, everyone was celebrating. It was the wrong time to break the news to the people that their prince couldn't give them what they wanted.'

Holly sank her hands into her hair, struggling to take in what he was saying. 'Who told you?'

'The doctor who treated me.'

'Well, the doctor was wrong.' Her hands fell to her sides and she walked across to him, her tone urgent. 'Look at me, Casper. *Listen* to me. Whatever you may have been told—whatever you think—you are not infertile. I *am* having your baby.'

'Don't do this, Holly.' He drew away from her. 'I've accepted your child as mine, and that's all that matters. You've given me my heir. The public think you're a genius.' He stared into his drink. 'At some point, I'll have to tell the people the truth. Let them decide about the succession.'

As the implications of his words sank in, Holly shook her head, horrified by what that would mean. 'No. You mustn't do that.'

'Because your newfound popularity would take a nosedive?' He gave a cynical smile. 'You think Santallia might rather not know that its new innocent princess has rather more sexual experience than they'd like?'

'Casper, my sexual experience encompasses you and only you.' Frustrated that she couldn't get through to him, Holly turned away and walked over to the window. Dawn was breaking and the rising sun sent pink shadows over the sea, but she saw nothing except her child's future crumbling before her. 'You should see a doctor again. You should have more tests. They made a mistake.'

'The subject is closed.'

'Fine. Don't have tests, then.' Anger and frustration rose out of her misery. 'But don't you *dare* announce to the world that this isn't your baby!' Her eyes suddenly fierce, she turned on him. 'I do *not* want our child having that sort of scar on his background. And once you've said something like that, you can never take it back.'

'They have a right to know about the baby's paternity.'

Holly straightened her shoulders. 'Once the baby is born, I'll prove our baby's paternity. Until then, you say nothing.'

'If you're so confident about paternity, then why wait? There are tests that can be done now. Or are you buying yourself more time?'

She lifted her hands to her cheeks, so stressed that she could hardly breathe. 'Tests now would put the baby at risk and I won't do that. But don't you dare tell anyone this isn't your baby. *Promise me, Casper.*'

'All right.'

Celebrating that minor victory, Holly sank onto the curved window seat and stared down at the sea lapping at the white sand below. 'Why didn't you tell me this when we were in London?'

'Because you didn't need to know.'

'How can you say that?'

'You wanted a father for your baby and I needed an heir. The details were irrelevant and they still are. You have a prince, a palace and a fortune. This drama is unnecessary.'

'I wanted our baby to know its father,' Holly whispered softly, her hand covering her abdomen in an instinctive gesture of protection. 'I thought marrying you *was* the right thing to do.'

'If it's any consolation, I wouldn't have let you make any other decision. And I don't want to talk about this again, Holly. You'll have everything you need and so will the baby.'

No. No, she wouldn't.

Holly closed her eyes, trying to ignore the raw wound caused by his admission that the whole day had been a lie.

She'd felt lonely before, but nothing had come close to the feeling of isolation that engulfed her following Casper's rejection.

She desperately wanted to talk to someone—to confide.

But there was no one.

She was alone.

Except that she wasn't really alone, was she? She had their baby to think about—to protect.

Once he or she was born, she'd be able to prove that Casper was the father. And until then she just had to try and keep their hopelessly unstable little family unit together.

That was all that mattered.

Starved of affection from Casper and desperately worried about the future, Holly threw herself into palace life and her royal duties.

She spent hours pouring over a map until she was familiar with every part of Santallia. Determined to develop the knowledge of a local, she persuaded Emilio to drive her round. The result was that she shocked and delighted the public by her frequent impromptu appearances. Oblivious to security or protocol, she talked to everyone, finding out what they liked and how they felt.

And one thing that always came across was how much they loved Casper.

'You're just what he needs,' one old lady said as Holly sat by her bed in the hospital, keeping her company for half an hour after an exhausting morning of official visits. 'After the accident we thought he wouldn't recover, you know.'

Holly reached forward to adjust the old lady's pillows. 'You mean because he was so badly injured?'

'No. Because he lost so much. But now he has you to love.'

But he didn't want love, did he?

Holly managed a smile. 'I need to go. Tonight it's dinner with a president and his wife, no less. Do you want more tea before I go?'

'I want you to tell me about the state visit. What will you be wearing?'

'Actually, I'm not sure.' Holly thought about her extensive wardrobe. No one could accuse Casper of being stingy, she thought ruefully. The trouble was, she now had such a

variety of gorgeous designer clothes that choosing had
become impossible, but even that wasn't a problem, because
she now had someone to do it for her. When she'd first
realised that a member of staff had been employed purely to
keep her wardrobe in order and help her select outfits, she'd
gaped at Casper.

'You mean it's someone's whole job just to tell me how to
dress?'

He'd dismissed her amazement with a frown. 'How else
will you know what to wear for the various occasions? Her
job is to research every engagement in advance and make the
appropriate choice of outfit. It will stop you making an embarrassing mistake.'

The news that he found her potentially embarrassing had
done nothing for Holly's fragile confidence, and she'd humbly
accepted the woman's help.

Thinking of it, Holly smiled at the old lady. 'I think I'm
wearing a blue dress. With silver straps. A bit Hollywood, but
apparently the president loves glamour.'

'You're so beautiful, he'll be charmed. And blue is a good
colour for you. I've been admiring your bracelet—I had one
almost exactly like that when I was your age.' The woman's
eyes misted. 'My husband gave it to me because he said it was
the same colour as my eyes. I lost it years ago. Not that it
matters. The trouble with getting old is you don't have the
same opportunities to dress up.'

'You don't need an occasion,' Holly said blithely, slipping
the bracelet off and sliding it onto the old lady's bony wrist.
'There. It looks gorgeous.'

'You can't give me that.'

'Why not? It looks pretty on you. I must go or they'll start
moaning at me. Try not to seduce any of the doctors.' Holly
rose to her feet, silently acknowledging that part of her was re-

luctant to return to the palace. She loved visiting everyone and chatting. When she was out and about and talking to people, it was easier to pretend that she wasn't desperately lonely.

That her marriage wasn't empty.

Casper seemed to think that presents were a reasonable substitute for his company.

It had taken only a couple of days for her to discover that he set himself a punishing work schedule, spending much of the day involved in state business or royal engagements.

Since their wedding they'd spent virtually no daylight hours alone together. Every evening there seemed to be yet another formal banquet, foreign dignitaries to be entertained, another evening of smiles and polite conversation.

And the fact that he never saw her was presumably intentional, she thought miserably as she said her farewells to all the ladies on the ward and allowed Emilio to guide her back to the car.

Casper didn't want to spend time with her, did he?

All he wanted from the relationship was a hostess and someone with whom to enjoy a few exhausting hours of turbo-powered, high-octane sex every night.

He wasn't interested in anything else. Not conversation. Not even a hug. *Certainly* not a hug.

Holly slid into the back of the car, waving to the crowd who had gathered. *What would they say,* she wondered, *if they knew their handsome prince had never spent a whole night with her?*

He just took her to bed, had sex and then disappeared somewhere, as if he was afraid that lingering might encourage her to say something that he didn't want to hear.

Did he have another woman? Was that where he went when he left their bed?

To someone else?

Casper had a seemingly inexhaustible sex drive, and

Holly was well aware that there had been another woman in his life when he'd first met her in England. One of the papers had mentioned some European princess, and another a supermodel.

Were they still on the scene?

Feeling mentally and physically exhausted, Holly rested her head on the back seat of the limousine and promptly fell asleep.

She woke at Emlio's gentle insistence, walked into her beautiful bedroom with the view to die for and flopped down on her huge, fabulous bed.

Just five minutes, she promised herself.

Five minutes, then she'd have a shower and get ready for the evening.

Simmering with impatience after a long and incredibly frustrating day of talks with the president and the foreign minister, Casper strode through to the private wing of the palace.

In his pocket was an extravagant diamond necklace, designed for him by the world's most exclusive jeweller who had assured him that any woman presented with such an exquisite piece would know she was loved.

Casper had frowned at that, because love played no part in the relationship he had with Holly. But she was doing an excellent job fulfilling her role as princess. She deserved to be appreciated.

And this was why she'd married him, wasn't it?

For the benefits that he could offer her.

Contemplating her reaction to such a generous gift, a faint smile touched his mouth, and he mentally prepared himself for a stimulating evening.

Lost in a private fantasy which involved Holly, the diamonds and very little else, Casper strolled into his private sanctuary.

The first thing that hit him was the unusual silence.

Silence, he reflected with a degree of wry humour, had become something of a scarcity since he'd married Holly.

First there was the singing. She sang to herself as they were getting ready for the evening. She sang in the shower, she sang as she dressed, she even sang as she did her make-up. And if she wasn't singing she was talking, apparently determined to fill every moment of the limited time they had alone together with details about her day. Who she'd spoken to, what they'd said in return—she was endlessly fascinated by every small detail about the people she'd met.

In fact silence was such an alien thing since Holly had entered his life, that he noticed the absence of sound like others would notice the presence of a large elephant in the room.

Slightly irritated that she obviously hadn't yet returned from her afternoon of visits, Casper removed his tie with a few deft flicks of his fingers while swiftly scanning his private mail.

Finding it strangely hard to concentrate without background noise, he had to force himself to focus while he scribbled instructions for his private secretary. Intending to take a quick shower while waiting for Holly to return, he took the stairs up to the bedroom suite.

Holly lay still on the bed, fully clothed, as if she'd fallen there and not moved since. Her glorious hair tumbled unrestricted around her narrow shoulders and her eyes were closed, her dark lashes serving to accentuate the extreme pallor of her cheeks.

In the process of unbuttoning his shirt, Casper stilled.

His first reaction was one of surprise, because she was blessed with boundless energy and enthusiasm and he'd never before seen her sleeping during the day.

His second reaction was concern.

Knowing that she was an extremely light sleeper, he waited for her to sense his presence and stir. Contemplating the feminine curve of her hip, he felt an immediate surge of arousal, and decided that the best course of action would be to join her on the bed and wake her personally.

Glancing at his watch, he calculated that if they limited the foreplay they would still make dinner with the president.

He dispensed with his shirt, his eyes fixed on the creamy skin visible at the neckline of her flowery dress. *Stunning*, he thought to himself, and settled himself on the edge of the bed, ready to dedicate the next half hour to making her *extremely* happy.

But she didn't stir.

Disconcerted by her lack of response, Casper reached out a hand and touched her throat, feeling a rush of relief as he felt warm flesh and a steady pulse under his fingertips.

What had he expected?

Unsettled by the sudden absence of logic that had driven him to take the pulse of a sleeping woman, he withdrew his hand and rose to his feet, struggling against an irrational desire to pick up the phone and demand the immediate presence of a skilled medical team.

She was just tired, he assured himself, casting another long look in her direction. Acting on impulse, he reached down and gently removed her shoes. Then he stared at her dress and tried to work out whether it was likely to impede her rest in any way. For the first time in his life, a decision eluded him. Did he remove it and risk waking her, or leave it and risk her being uncomfortable?

A stranger to prevarication, Casper stood in a turmoil of indecision, his hand hovering over her for several long minutes. In the end he compromised by pulling the silk cover over her body.

Then he backed away from the bed, relieved that at least there had been no one present to witness such embarrassing vacillation on his part.

He made thousands of decisions on a daily basis, some of them involving millions of pounds, some of them involving millions of people.

It was incomprehensible that he couldn't make one small decision that affected his wife's comfort.

Holly awoke to darkness. With a rush of inexplicable panic, she sat up and only then did she notice Casper seated by the window.

'What time is it?' Disorientated and fuzzy headed, she reached across to flick on the lamp by the bed. 'It must be really late. And I need to change for dinner.'

'It's one in the morning. You've missed dinner.'

The lamp sent a shaft of light across the room, and she saw that his white dress-shirt was unbuttoned at the throat and that his dinner jacket was slung carelessly over the back of the chair.

'I missed it?' Holly slid her hand through her hair, trying to clear her head. 'How could I have missed it?'

'You were asleep.'

'Then you should have woken me.' Mortified, she pushed down the luxurious silk bed cover and realised that she was still wearing the clothes she'd had on when she'd done her day of royal visits. 'I only wanted a short nap.'

'Holly, you slept as though you were dead.' His dark eyes glittered in the subtle light. 'I decided that it was better to make your excuses to the president than produce a wife in a coma.'

Holly pulled a face. 'What must he have thought?'

'He thought you were pregnant,' Casper drawled, a faint smile touching his mouth. 'He and his wife have four children, and he spent the entire evening lecturing me on how a pregnant woman often feels most tired during the first few months and how rest is important.'

'God, how awful for you,' Holly mumbled, forcing herself

to get out of bed even though every part of herself was dying to lie down and sleep for the rest of the night. 'I feel really bad, because I know how important this dinner was to you. Your private secretary told me that you wanted to talk about all that trade stuff and about carbon emissions or something. Some forestry scheme?'

A strange expression flickered across his face. 'You frequently talk to my private secretary?'

'Of course.' Holly tried unsuccessfully to suppress a yawn as she padded over to him in bare feet. 'Carlos and I often talk. How else am I going to know what the point of the evening is? I mean, you don't see these people because you like their company, do you?' Feeling decidedly wobbly, she sank down on the window seat next to him. 'I'm sorry I slept.'

'Don't be. Though I must admit you had me worried for a while. It wasn't until I was greeted with silence that I realised how accustomed I am to hearing you singing into a hairbrush.'

Holly turned scarlet at the thought that he'd witnessed that. 'You hear me singing?'

'The whole of the palace hears you singing.'

Horrified by that disclosure, Holly shrank back on the seat. 'I didn't know anyone could hear me,' she muttered. 'Singing always cheers me up.'

His eyes lingered thoughtfully on her face. 'Do you need cheering up?'

How was she supposed to answer that? Holly hesitated, knowing that if she told him that she felt lonely, *that she missed him*, he'd withdraw in the same way he always did when she made a move towards him. He'd remind her that his company wasn't part of their 'deal'.

'I just like singing,' she said lamely. 'But next time I'll make sure no one is listening.'

'That would be a pity, especially given that several of the staff have told me what a beautiful voice you have.' He reached into his pocket and withdrew a slim box. 'I bought you a present.'

'Oh.' She tried to look pleased. After all, he was trying, wasn't he? It wouldn't be fair to point out that her wardrobes were bulging with clothes and that she only had one pair of feet on which to wear shoes, and that what she *really* wanted was a few hours in his company when they weren't having sex. 'Thank you.'

'I hope you like it.' His confident smile suggested that he wasn't in any doubt about that, and Holly flipped open the lid of the dark-blue velvet box and was dazzled by the sparkle and gleam of diamonds.

'My goodness.'

'They're pink diamonds. I know you like pink. Apparently they're very rare.'

When had he even noticed that she liked pink?

He was such a contradiction, she thought numbly, lifting the necklace from the box and instantly falling in love with it. He spent hardly any time alone with her, but he seemed to be trying to please her.

And he'd noticed that she liked pink.

'It's beautiful,' she said honestly, fastening the necklace round her neck and walking across the room to admire herself in the mirror. 'Is it very valuable?'

'Would knowing how much it cost make it a more welcome gift?' There was an edge to his tone that she didn't understand.

'No, of course not.' She touched the sparkling diamonds nervously. 'I'm just wondering whether I dare wear it out of the bedroom.'

He relaxed slightly. 'It's yours to lose, keep or trade,' he drawled softly, and Holly frowned, puzzled by his comment but too tired to search for a hidden meaning.

'You do say the weirdest things.' Suppressing a yawn, she

walked back to the window seat, feeling the weight of the diamonds against her throat. 'I've never worn diamonds before. And I never imagined wearing them in bed.'

'I intended them to go with your dress this evening.' His gaze was fixed on her face. 'You're extremely tired.'

'Long day.'

'Too long. The official visits have to stop, Holly.'

'What? *Why?*' Hurt and upset by the apparent criticism, Holly sat up straighter in her seat. 'What am I doing wrong? I've worked so hard.'

'Precisely. You're working too hard.'

For a moment Holly just gaped at him in disbelief. 'That's the most unfair criticism I've ever heard. How can I be working *too* hard?'

'If you're so exhausted you're falling asleep, then you're working too hard.'

'That's nothing to do with the official visits. I'm falling asleep because you keep me awake half the night!' She looked at him in exasperation, her temper mounting. 'Oh, that's it, isn't it? You don't like me working hard because you're afraid I'm going to be too tired to perform in the bedroom! Is that all you care about, Casper? Whether I have the energy for sex?'

'You're doing that uniquely female thing of twisting words for the purpose of starting a row.' Ice cool, he watched her with masculine detachment and Holly felt a flash of frustration.

'No, I'm not. I *hate* rows. I would never, ever choose to row with anyone. I *hate* conflict.' The ironic gleam in his eyes somehow served to make her even more infuriated. 'And you'd know I hate conflict if you'd bothered to spend a few hours alone in my company! But you don't, do you? Do you realise we've never even been on a proper date? You are so, so selfish! You just come to bed and do your whole virile, macho-stud thing, and then you swan off, leaving me.'

One dark brow lifted in cool appraisal. 'Leaving you?'

'Exhausted,' she muttered, and a sardonic smile touched his mouth.

'So I leave you to sleep. By my definition, that makes me unselfish, not selfish. And it brings me back to my earlier point, which is that you're working too hard.'

'You always have to win, don't you?' Holly sank back down onto the window seat, the bout of anger having sapped the last of her energy. It just wasn't worth arguing with him.

'It isn't about winning. Believe it or not, I do have your welfare at heart. After I left you this afternoon, I asked a few questions. Questions I should have asked a long time ago it seems.' There was a frown in his eyes. 'It's no wonder you're so tired. Apparently you've been working flat out since the day after our wedding. You've been doing ten to fifteen visits a day! And you spend ages with everyone. From what I've been told, you don't even give yourself a lunch break.'

'Well, there's a lot to fit in.' Holly defended herself. 'Have you any idea how many requests the palace receives? People send letters, sometimes official and sometimes handwritten. Stacks and stacks of them. There have already been requests for me to go and visit schools and hospitals, open this or that, make an official visit, cut ribbons, smash bottles of champagne—I judged a dog show last week and I don't know *anything* about dogs. And then there are the individuals, people who are ill and can't get out—'

'Holly.' His tone was a mixture of amusement and disbelief. 'You're not supposed to say yes to all of them. The idea is that you pick and choose.'

'Well if I say yes to one and not another then I'm going to offend someone!' Holly glared at him and then subsided. 'And anyway, I'm enjoying myself. I like seeing people. For some reason that I absolutely don't understand, it cheers them up to see me. And I won't give it up!'

People liked her. People approved of her.

She felt as though she was making a difference, and it felt good.

'You're working yourself to the bone. From now on I'm giving instructions that you're to do no more than two engagements a day,' he instructed. 'On a maximum of five days a week.'

'No!' Horrified by that prospect, Holly pushed her hair out of her eyes. 'What am I going to do the rest of the time? You obviously don't want to see me during the hours of daylight, you're—you're like a vampire or something! You just turn up at night.'

Thick dark lashes concealed his expression. 'You have unlimited funds and virtually unlimited opportunities for entertainment.' His soft drawl connected straight with her nerve endings, and Holly felt everything weaken.

'Well there's no point in doing stuff if you don't have anyone to share it with. I'm lonely. And that's the other thing you don't seem to understand about me. I'm a people person. So don't tell me I have to stop doing my own engagements.'

'Holly, you're exhausted.'

'I'm pregnant,' she said flatly, pulling her legs under her and trying hard to hide another yawn. 'All the books say that in another couple of weeks I'll be bounding with energy.'

'And what are you going to do then?' His tone was dry. 'Work nights?'

Her eyes collided with his and Holly sucked in some air, horrified to discover that the mere mention of the word 'night' was sufficient to trigger a reaction in her body. Her nipples tightened, her pelvis ached and she suddenly felt as though she'd downed an entire bottle of champagne in one gulp.

Clearly tracking the direction of her thoughts, he gave a slow, confident smile and suddenly she wanted to thump him because he was unreasonably, unfairly gorgeous, and he knew it.

As his gaze welded to her mouth, Holly acknowledged the overwhelming surge of excitement with something close to despair. '*Don't* look at me like that. You're doing it again— all you think about is sex.'

'And what are you thinking about right now, *tesoro*? The share price?' His tone was mocking as he pulled her gently but firmly to her feet. 'A new handbag?'

A moan of disbelief escaped her parted lips as he brought his mouth down on hers and backed her purposefully towards the bed.

This was Casper at his most dominant and she really, *really* wanted to be able tell him that she was too tired, or just not interested.

'I can't believe you make me feel this way.' Her body exploded under the hard, virile pressure of his and she tumbled back onto the mattress, forced to admit that she was a lost cause when it came to resisting him.

She wanted him *so* much.

And if this was all their relationship was…

He came over her with the fluid assurance of a male who has never known rejection, arousal glittering in his beautiful eyes. 'Exactly how tired are you?'

Trying to look nonchalant, she shrugged. 'Why do you ask?'

He lowered his arrogant, dark head, his mouth curving into a sardonic smile as it hovered close to hers. 'Because I'm about to do my virile, macho-stud thing,' he mocked gently, and Holly felt her stomach flip with desperate excitement.

Weak with desire, *hating* herself for being so feeble where he was concerned, she gasped as his hand slid under the silk of her nightdress. 'Casper.'

His hand stilled and there was a wicked gleam in his eyes. 'Unless you're too tired?'

Driven by the desperate urgency of her body, Holly swallowed her pride. 'I'm not *that* tired…'

'You have time to shower while I make some calls.' Freshly shaved, his hair still damp, Casper straightened his silk tie and reached for his jacket. 'I'll join you for breakfast.'

Elated that he'd spent the entire night with her for the first time, and reluctant to risk disturbing the fragile shoots of their relationship, Holly decided not to confess that mornings weren't her best time and that she couldn't touch breakfast.

Waiting until he'd left the room, she slid cautiously out of bed, felt her stomach heave alarmingly and just made it to the bathroom in time.

'*Dio,* what is the matter?' Casper's voice came from right behind her. 'Are you ill? Is it something you ate?'

'Don't you knock? I thought I locked the door.' Mortified that he should witness her at her lowest, Holly leaned her head against the cool tiles, willing her stomach to settle. 'Please, Casper, show a little sensitivity and go away.'

'First you accuse me of not spending time with you, then you want me to go away.' Casper lifted his hands in a gesture of frustrated incredulity. 'Make up your mind!'

'Well, *obviously* I don't want you around while I'm being sick!'

'You're incredibly pale.' Looking enviably fit and impossibly handsome, he frowned down at her. 'I'm calling a doctor.'

'Casper.' She gritted her teeth, terrified that she'd be ill in front of him. 'It's fine. It happens all the time. It will fade in a minute.'

'*What* happens all the time?' His dark gaze was fixed on her face, the tension visible in his powerful shoulders. 'I've never seen you like this before.'

'That's because you're never here in the morning,' she muttered, wondering what cruel twist of fate had made him decide to pick this particular morning to linger in her company. 'You go to bed with me, but you choose to wake up somewhere else.' *With someone else.* The words were left unsaid, but a gleam of sardonic humour flickered in his very sexy dark eyes.

'You think I spend half the night making love with you and then move on to the next woman? A sort of sexual conveyor-belt, perhaps?'

'I honestly don't want to know where you go at three in the morning.' She gave a moan as another wave of nausea washed over her. 'Oh, go away, please. I don't even care at the moment—I can't *believe* you're seeing me like this. You're never going to find me sexy again.'

'There is not the slightest chance of that happening.' After a moment's hesitation he dropped to his haunches and stroked her hair away from her face with a surprisingly gentle hand. 'I am sorry you feel ill. Wash your face. It will make you feel better.' He stood up, dampened a towel and wiped it gently over her face.

'I already feel better. It passes.' She sat back on her heels and gave him a wobbly smile. 'I bet you're regretting all those times you could have stayed the whole night and had breakfast with me. I'm thrilling company in the morning, don't you think?'

With a wry smile, he lifted her easily to her feet. 'Does food help? If I suggested something to eat would you hit me?'

'I've never been an advocate of violence.' It felt weird, having a conversation with him that wasn't based on conflict. And frustrating that they were having it when she was still in her nightdress.

But at least she was wearing diamonds, she thought wryly. Conscious of his sleek good looks and her own undressed state, Holly glanced towards the shower. 'I think I'd like a shower. Do I still have time?'

'Yes. But don't lock the door.' His tone was gruff. 'I don't want you collapsing.'

'I'm fine.' This new level of attentiveness was unsettling. There was a shift in their relationship that she didn't understand.

But she knew better than to read anything into it.

She showered quickly, selected a cream skirt from her wardrobe and added a tailored jacket that allowed a peep of her pretty camisole. She scooped her hair up and then had a moment of agonising indecision as she remembered that he seemed to prefer her hair down. Up or down? Removing the clips, her hair tumbled around her shoulders in a mass of soft curls.

Deciding that she should have left it up, she started to twist it again and then caught herself.

What was she doing? For crying out loud, she was going to eat breakfast with the man, that was all. It wasn't a formal dinner or a state occasion. Just breakfast.

Pathetic, she told her reflection. Absolutely pathetic.

It was just for the baby. For the baby's sake she wanted them to have a happy, successful marriage.

Afraid to examine that theory too closely in case it fell apart, she walked onto the terrace to join him for breakfast. Casper was talking on the phone, looking lean and sleek, his hips resting casually against the balustrade that circled the pretty balcony. Behind him stretched the ocean, the early-morning sunlight catching the surface in a thousand dazzling lights.

The billionaire prince, she thought weakly, envious of his confidence and the ease with which he handled his high profile existence. She'd watched him in action at state occasions and been impossibly awed by the deft way in which he handled every situation and solved every problem. She realised now that she'd had no idea of the weight of responsibility that rested on him, and yet he apparently coped easily, with no outward evidence of stress or self-doubt.

As he continued his conversation, his eyes slid to hers and held. Electricity jolted her and Holly's heart bumped hard against her ribs.

Wondering how he could have this effect on her when she'd just spent most of the night in bed with him, she plopped down onto the nearest chair.

She felt light-headed and dizzy and wasn't sure whether to blame pregnancy, lack of food or the shattering impact of the extremely sexy man who was currently watching her with disturbing intensity, apparently paying no attention whatsoever to the person on the other end of the phone.

Cheeks pink, trying to distract herself, Holly cautiously examined the food that had been laid out on the table.

Terminating the call, Casper dropped his phone into his pocket and strolled across to her. 'I've talked to the doctor.'

'You have?'

'He suggests that you eat dry toast now. And tomorrow you're to eat a dry biscuit before you move from the bed.'

'That sounds exciting. And guaranteed to put on extra pounds just when I don't need them.'

Casper gave a predatory smile. 'Since we've already established the positive impact of biscuits on a certain part of your anatomy, I think we can safely assume that I'm not going to find you sexually repulsive any time soon.'

'I didn't say you were.'

'But you were thinking it.' He sat down opposite her and helped himself to fresh fruit. 'Eventually I'm hoping you'll realise that you have a fabulous body. Then we can make love with the lights on. Or even during daylight.'

She blushed, as self-conscious about his suggestion that

they make love in daylight as she was flattered by his comments about her body. 'You're not around during the day.'

'The promise of you naked would be sufficient incentive to persuade me to ditch my responsibilities.'

'All you think about is sex. I don't know whether to be flattered or exasperated.'

'You should be flattered. I'm a man. I'm programmed to think about nothing but sex.' Apparently seeing nothing wrong in that admission, he reached across and lifted the coffee pot. 'More?'

Holly pulled a face and shook her head. 'I've gone off it. Don't ask me why. Something to do with being pregnant, I think.'

Without arguing, he poured her a fresh orange-juice instead. 'And now I want to know why you assumed I was spending part of the night with another woman.'

Her insides tumbled. 'Well—it just seemed like the obvious answer.'

'To what question?'

'To where you go at three in the morning. Up until today, you've never woken up next to me. We have sex. You leave. That's the routine.'

'That doesn't explain why you'd believe I was seeing another woman.'

'You're a man.' She mimicked his tone, hoping that her attempt at humour would conceal the fact that she was absolutely terrified of his answer. 'And that's what men are programmed to do.'

'I get up at three in the morning because I'm aware that you need some sleep,' he said softly. 'And if I'm in bed with you I don't seem to have any self-control.'

Stunned by that unexpected confession, Holly felt her insides flip. 'But by the time you leave the bed we've already—' Her cheeks heated. 'I mean surely even you couldn't?'

'I definitely could,' he assured her silkily. 'It seems where you're concerned, I have a limitless appetite. So you see, *tesoro*, you don't have to worry about the effects of daylight, biscuits, or anything else for that matter. I'm so addicted to your body I even find you sexy in a cartoon tee-shirt—not that I'd ever allow you to wear one of those again,' he went on, clearly concerned she might decide to put that claim to the test.

Basking in the novel experience of being considered irresistible, Holly sipped her orange juice. He didn't reveal anything about his own emotions and they didn't talk about their problems, but they seemed to have reached some sort of truce. 'So where *do* you go when you leave our bed?'

'I work. Usually in the study.'

Holly gave a disbelieving laugh because that altogether more simple explanation hadn't occurred to her. 'I just assumed— The thing is, I've been so worried.' Weak with relief, she confessed, 'I mean, I know you had loads of relationships before me.'

'I sense this is turning into one of those female questions where every answer is always going to be the wrong one,' he drawled and she bit her lip.

'But—were you with someone when we met at the rugby?'

'Technically, no.'

'What's that supposed to mean? I read about a super-model—'

'You don't want to believe everything you read.'

'But —'

His tone was impatient. 'What can you possibly gain from this line of questioning?'

Reassurance? She gave a painful laugh as she realised the foolishness of that. Reassurance about what—that he loved her? He didn't. She knew he didn't. 'I was just—interested.'

'You were just being a woman. Forget it.' He rose to his feet. 'Remember that the past is always behind you. Are you ready?'

'For what?' She decided that this wasn't the right time to

point out that the past wasn't behind him, even if he believed that it was. It was obvious to her that it was with him every agonising minute of the day. 'Where are we going?'

His gaze lingered on her face. 'To spend some time together. Isn't that what you wanted? You said that I don't spend any time with you during the day,' he reminded her softly. 'And that we've never actually been on a date. So we're going to rectify that.'

'We're going on a date?' Holly couldn't stop the smile. 'Where?'

'The most romantic city in the world. Rome.'

CHAPTER SEVEN

'THIS is your idea of a date? When you said we were visiting romantic Rome, I imagined wandering hand in hand to the Spanish Steps and the Colosseum. Not sitting in a rugby stadium,' Holly muttered, taking her seat and waving enthusiastically to the very vocal crowd.

Casper gave her a rare smile. 'You wanted to be alone with me. We're alone.'

'This is your idea of alone?' Holly glanced at the security team surrounding them, and then at the enormous crowd who were cheering as the players jogged onto the pitch. 'Are you delusional?'

'Stadio Flaminio is a small stadium—intimate.'

Holly started to laugh. 'I suppose everything is relative. It's small compared with Twickenham. This time we're only in the company of thirty thousand people. But is this really your idea of romantic? A rugby match?'

'We met during a rugby match,' Casper reminded her, and their eyes clashed as both of them remembered the sheer breathless intensity of that meeting. 'I am mixing my two passions. Rugby and you.'

He didn't actually mean *her*, did he? He meant her body.

'I—I've never actually watched a game before,' Holly confessed shakily, dragging her eyes from his and wondering what it was about him that reduced her to jelly. 'I was always working. I don't even know the rules.'

'One team has to score more points than the other,' Casper said dryly, leaning forward as the game started, his gaze intent on the pitch.

'By all piling on top of each other?' Holly winced as she watched the players throw themselves into the game with no apparent care for their own safety. 'It's all very macho, isn't it? Lots of mud, blood and muscle.'

'They're following strict rules. Watch. You might find it exciting.'

And she did.

At first she sat in silence, determined not to ruin his enjoyment by asking inane questions, and equally determined to try and understand what he loved about the game. But, far from ignoring her, he seemed keen to involve her in everything that was going on.

There was a sudden roar from the crowd as a man powered down the field with the ball.

'He's fast,' Holly breathed, and Casper's shoulders tensed and then he punched the air.

'He's scored the opening try.'

'That's when he puts the ball down on the line—and that's five points, right?'

Casper was absorbed in the game, but not too absorbed to make the occasional observation for her benefit. Gradually he explained the rules, until the game no longer looked like a playground fight fuelled by testosterone, and instead became an extremely exciting sporting challenge.

Towards the second half of the match Holly discovered that she was leaning forward too, her eyes on the pitch, equally absorbed by what was happening. 'That was a brilliant run through the Italian defence.' Turning to find Casper watching her, she blushed. 'What? Did I say something stupid?'

'No.' His voice was husky and there was a strange light in his eyes. 'You are quite right. It *was* a brilliant run by England. You are enjoying yourself?'

'Very much.' She gave a tentative smile, and turned back to the pitch. 'That tackle was by the Italian hooker, is that right?' Suddenly aware that the sun was shining down on them, and she was far too hot, she released a few buttons on her jacket. 'I can't believe they named a rugby position after a prostitute.'

'They are called hookers because they use their feet to hook the ball in the scrum. They're a key…' His voice tailed off in the middle of the sentence, and all his attention was suddenly focused on the delicate lace of her camisole. 'Sorry, what was the question?' He dragged his gaze up to hers, his eyes suddenly blank, and she gave a feminine smile.

'You were teaching me about rugby.'

'If you really want to learn,' he breathed, leaning closer to her, 'Don't start undressing in the middle of my answer.'

'I was hot.'

He gave a wry smile. 'So am I.'

Delighted by the effect she was having on him, her eyes sparkled. 'Where were we? Oh yes—you were telling me about the hooker.'

He stroked a finger over her cheek. 'Unless you want to find yourself participating in an indecent act in a public place,' he purred, 'I suggest you stop teasing. And the hooker is a key position in attacking and defensive play.'

Suddenly she wished they were somewhere more private. 'So you played rugby at school and university, is that right?' Swiftly she changed the subject. 'That's how you know the England captain?'

'He has been a close friend of mine for years.'

And watching rugby was probably one of the few occasions when he could switch off and forget he was a prince, Holly thought to herself as they both settled down to watch the game again.

The match ended with an England victory, and Casper and Holly joined the players at the post-match reception.

Casper was guest of honour and gave a short, humorous speech that had everyone laughing. Watching him mingle with the players and guests afterwards, Holly was fascinated by the change in him. As he smoothly and skilfully dealt with all the people who wanted to speak to him, there was no sign of the icily reserved man she'd been living with, and in his place was the confident, charismatic prince who had seduced her.

But this was his public persona, she reminded herself.

He switched on the charm and gave them what they expected.

But at what personal sacrifice?

He'd buried his own needs for those of other people.

And now he was laughing with the England captain, his old friend, and Holly pushed aside darker thoughts as he introduced her.

'You look different without the mud,' she confessed naïvely, and the man lifted her hand to his lips with laughter in his eyes.

'So you're the woman who distracted me at Twickenham. There I was, focusing on the ball, trying to block out the world around me, and suddenly Royal Boy here is kissing this stunning woman.'

Holly blushed. 'You've known each other a long time.'

'I know all his secrets, but I wouldn't dare tell.' The man grinned. 'He's bigger and tougher than me.'

Holly's eyes slid to Casper's broad shoulders and she reflected on the fact that his physique was every bit as impressive as this man who was a sporting hero to millions. Her stomach squirmed with longing and she felt herself blushing as her eyes met his questioning gaze.

'I really enjoyed the game,' she said hastily. 'Thanks for taking me.'

The England captain punched Casper on the arm. 'I can understand why you married her. Any woman who thanks you for taking them to a game of rugby has got to be worth hanging onto.' He winked. 'And it helps that she looks gorgeous.'

'All right, enough.' Casper curved an arm around Holly's shoulders in an unmistakeably possessive gesture. 'Time for you to go and charm someone else.'

Finally they were escorted to the waiting limousine, and Holly slid inside. 'I really envy the fact that when you speak all the words come out in the right order.'

Casper's glance was amused. 'And that's surprising?'

'Well, I'm all right with words generally, but in a tricky situation they never come out the way I want them too. I always think of the right thing to say about four days after the opportunity to say it has passed. And I'm *hopeless* at standing up for myself because I hate conflict. The moment anyone glares at me I just want them to stop being angry, and the words tie themselves in knots in my mouth.'

'You stood up to me that day in your friend's flat.'

'That was an exception,' she muttered. 'You were saying awful things to me, none of them true. Generally if someone yells at me I turn into a mute.' The car sped through the centre of Rome, negotiating the clog of traffic and tourists.

'No matter how hard I try, I can't imagine you as a mute,' Casper said dryly, and Holly shrugged.

'I envy your confidence. I've never had much of that.' She studied his profile. 'You must miss the days when you could just go to rugby matches and spend time with your friends.

Was it hard for you—becoming the ruling prince? I mean, it wasn't what you expected, was it?'

For a moment he didn't answer, then his mouth tightened slightly. 'The circumstances were hard.'

Had he just shut it away? she wondered. For eight years? If so, no wonder he seemed so cold and detached with her. He'd never given himself a chance to heal.

'Have you *ever* talked about it?' Concern for him made her bold. 'Sorry, but bottling it up for ever can't be a good thing.'

'Holly—'

'Sorry, sorry; OK, I won't ask again,' she said hastily. 'But do you think you could at least give me some detail about how your work evolved? It's just a bit embarrassing when people who have lived here all their lives say things to me and I have to look as though I know what they're talking about, while I really don't have a clue. Someone was praising you for your vision and courage—something to do with the way you transformed the way Santallia did things. I tried to look as though I knew what he was talking about, but obviously I didn't. I just thought it might help if you told me a bit about—things. I don't want to look thick.' Retreating slightly in her seat as she saw Casper lift long bronzed fingers to his forehead, she braced herself for the explosion of Mediterranean volatility that was inevitably going to follow a gesture of frank exasperation.

Surprisingly, when he looked at her there was laughter in his eyes. 'Has anyone ever told you you'd make an excellent torture weapon? You go on and on until a guy is ready to surrender.'

'It's just jolly hard to talk to people if you don't have all the information, and I don't happen to think silence is healthy,' Holly mumbled, and Casper gave a shake of his head.

'Fine. Tonight over dinner, I will outline the highlights of my life so far. And it's only fair to warn you that you'll be bored out of your mind.'

'We're having dinner? Don't tell me, there will be seven hundred other people there.'

'Just the two of us.'

'Just us?' A dark, dangerous thrill cramped her stomach. Perhaps finally, they'd have the opportunity to deepen their relationship. And she knew she wouldn't be bored hearing about his past. She was fast discovering that nothing about him bored her.

'Just us, Holly.' His voice was soft and his eyes lingered on her mouth. 'Late dinner. After our trip to the opera.'

'You're taking me to the opera? Seriously?'

'Given that you sing all the time, I thought you might enjoy it.'

In the darkened auditorium, Casper found himself focusing on Holly's face rather than the opera.

He could see the glisten of tears in her eyes as she responded to the emotional story being played out on the stage in front of them, and marvelled at how open she was with her feelings.

Since the curtain had risen, she'd appeared to have forgotten his existence, so lost was she in Mozart's score and the beauty of the singing.

Casper's eyes rested on the seductive curve of her shoulders, bared by the exquisite sequinned dress that appeared to be superglued to her exotic curves. Around the slender column of her neck were the pink diamonds, glittering against her smooth, pale skin.

From the tip of her simple satin shoes to the elegant coil of her newly straightened hair, she'd slipped into the role of princess with astonishing ease.

Their trip had somehow become public knowledge and, when their limousine had pulled up outside the opera house, a crowd had gathered hoping to see them.

But far from being daunted, or even disappointed that their 'private' evening had become public, she'd spent several minutes chatting, smiling and charming both the crowd and the photographers, until Casper had pointed out that they were going to miss the opera.

And when they'd walked into their box there had been no privacy because every head in the opera house had turned to gaze. Even now he was sure that half the audience were straining to catch a glimpse of his wife, rather than the soprano currently giving her all on the stage.

But Holly wasn't bothered.

He'd misjudged her, he admitted to himself, studying her profile in the darkness.

He'd thought that she would struggle with her new life.

But her only complaint was that he didn't spend enough time with her.

In the grip of a sudden surge of lust, Casper contemplated suggesting that they cut out during the interval, but he couldn't bring himself to do that because she was so obviously enjoying herself.

She was so enthusiastic about everything—meeting people, opera—even rugby.

Casper frowned slightly, admitting to himself that she'd surprised him. Over and over again. He'd expected her to struggle with the crowds and the attention but she'd responded like a professional. He'd thought she'd be tongue tied at official functions, but she was so warm and friendly that everyone was keen to engage her in conversation. He'd expected her to snap at him for dragging her to the rugby, but after the initial humour she'd shown as much interest and energy in that as she did with everything.

He remembered her comment about being lonely and his mind wandered back to the newspaper article that had revealed her pregnancy. At the time he'd been so angry, he hadn't paid attention.

But hadn't there been some revelation about her father?

'So this *palazzo* is owned by one of your friends?' Holly wandered onto the roof terrace, which felt like a slice of paradise in the centre of such a busy city. A profusion of exotic plants and flowers twisted around the ornate iron balustrade, and in the distance she could see the floodlit Colosseum. 'You certainly have influential friends.'

'It is more private than staying in a hotel, or as the guest of the President.'

For once they were guaranteed complete privacy, and that fact alone somehow increased the feeling of intimacy.

She'd wanted to be alone, but now that they were, she felt ridiculously self-conscious.

'I love the diamonds.' She touched her necklace and he smiled.

'They look good on you. I'm glad you didn't change.'

Aware that Casper had watched her more than the opera, Holly had opted to wear the same dress for dinner. The fact that he hadn't been able to take his eyes off her had been a heady experience.

'You like my dress?' Smoothing her hands over her hips in a typically feminine gesture, she glanced down at herself. 'It's not too clingy?'

'It's you I like,' he murmured, 'not the dress.' He stroked a hand over her shoulder and Holly decided that she might wear the dress for ever.

'All right, now this feels like being on a date,' she said, laughing nervously as she took the glass of champagne he was offering her. 'The weather is gorgeous. It's really warm, considering it's only March.'

'You finally have me alone, and our topic of conversation is going to be the weather?' Casper trailed appreciative dark eyes down her body. 'Has today tired you out?'

'No.' Her nerves on fire, she walked to the edge of the balcony and stared at the ruins of the Colosseum, reminding herself to be careful what she said. 'It's been fun. Thank you.'

'It's probably less tiring than the visits you've been doing. You're in the early stages of pregnancy. Your doctor told me that it can be an exhausting time. Most women in your position would have been lying in the sun with a book.'

'If I wasn't married to you, I'd be waiting tables, pregnant or not,' Holly said dryly, glancing at her luxurious, privileged surroundings with something close to disbelief. 'Being married to you isn't exactly tiring. Someone else makes all the arrangements and tells me where I need to be and when. I even have someone who suggests what I wear. Someone does my hair and make-up. I just turn up and chat to people.'

'And chatting is your favourite occupation. Are you hungry?' Amusement shimmered in his eyes as he steered her towards the table. Silver glinted and candles flickered, and the air was filled with the scent of flowers. 'I must admit I hadn't expected you to cope so well with all the attention. When I first met you, you seemed very insecure. I hadn't factored in how warm and friendly you are. You have a real talent with people.'

'I do?' Warmed by his unexpectedly generous praise, Holly glowed, smiling her thanks at a member of staff who discreetly placed a napkin on her lap. 'That's a nice thing to say.'

'Why were you a waitress?'

'What's wrong with being a waitress?'

'Don't be defensive.' He waited while a team of staff served their food and then dismissed them with a discreet glance towards the door. 'There's nothing wrong with being a waitress, but you could have done a great deal more. You're obviously very bright—even if maths isn't "your thing".'

'I've never been very ambitious.' Holly sipped her drink, wondering if honesty would destroy the atmosphere. 'I know it isn't trendy or politically correct to admit to it, but all I really wanted was to have a baby. When other girls wanted to be doctors or lawyers, I just wanted to be a mum. Not just any mum, but a brilliant mum. And before you say anything, yes, I suppose a psychologist would have a field day with that and say I wanted to make up for my parents' deficient parenting—but actually I don't think that had anything to do with it. I think I just have a very strong maternal instinct.'

'You're right, it isn't politically correct to admit that.' His eyes held hers. 'Most of the women I know think babies are something to be postponed until they've done all the other things in life.'

Not wanting to think about the women he knew, Holly looked away. 'I always saw children as a beginning, not as an end.' She glanced towards the open glass doors and saw several members of staff hovering. 'Do you think—could they just put the dishes on the table and leave us alone?'

She didn't even see him gesture and yet the staff melted away and the doors were closed, leaving them alone.

'I love it when you do that.' Holly grinned and picked up her fork. 'Do the whole powerful prince thing: "you are dismissed". Do you ever eat in restaurants?'

'Occasionally, but it usually causes too much of a security headache for all concerned. You enjoyed the opera, didn't you?'

'It was fantastic. The costumes, the music.' She sighed. 'Can we go again some time?'

'You've never been before? But you were living in London—a mecca for culture.'

'If you have money. And, even then, London can be a pretty lonely place,' Holly said lightly. 'Loads of people all going about their business, heads down, not looking left or right. I hated the anonymity of it—the fact that no one cared about anyone else. I always thought it would be great to live in a small village where everyone knows everyone, but I needed the work, and there's always work in a city.'

'You don't like being on your own, do you?'

Holly played with her fork. 'No. I suppose I was on my own a lot as a child and I hated it. After my dad left, my mum had to go out to work, and she couldn't afford childcare so she pretty much left me to my own devices. Then she died, and—' She poked at the food on her plate. 'Let's just say I don't associate being on my own with happy feelings. Screwed-up Holly.'

'You seem remarkably balanced to me, considering the state of the world around us.' He gave a faint smile. 'A little dreamy and naïve perhaps. Did you read fairy tales as a child?'

'What's that supposed to mean? I don't believe in fairies, if that's what you're asking me.'

'But you believe in love,' he drawled, curling his long fingers around the slender stem of his glass.

'Love isn't a fairy tale.'

'Isn't it?' The flickering candles illuminated the hard planes of his handsome face and the cynical glitter of his eyes.

'Do you realise how weird this is? I mean—you're the prince with the palace and you're telling me you don't believe in fairy tales. Bizarre.' Holly laughed. 'And, if you were already living out the fairy story, what did your nannies read you? Something about normal people?'

'I was swamped by literature drumming in the importance of responsibility and duty.'

Pondering that revealing statement, Holly studied him thoughtfully. 'So it was all about what your country needed.

Not about you as a person. What was your childhood like? Did it feel weird being a prince?'

'I've never been anything else, so I have no idea. But my childhood was pretty normal.' He leaned forward and topped up her glass. 'I was educated at home, and then went to boarding school in England, university in the States and then returned here to work on the tourist development programme.'

'Everyone says you did a brilliant job. Do you miss it?'

'I still keep my eye on all the projects. I'm probably more involved than I should be.' He was unusually communicative, and if Holly was only too aware that they weren't talking about any of the difficult stuff, well, she decided it didn't matter. At least they were talking about *something*. And at least they were alone together instead of surrounded by a crowd of dignitaries.

'I wish we could do this more often,' she said impulsively and then blushed as he rose from the table, a purposeful gleam in his eyes.

'We will. And now that's enough talking.' He pulled her gently to her feet and she stood, heart thumping, and he slid his hands around her face and gave an unexpected smile.

'For the rest of the evening,' he murmured softly, 'It's actions, not words. How does this spectacular dress come off?'

'Zip at the back,' Holly murmured, offering no resistance as he lowered his head to hers.

As always the skilled touch of his mouth sent her head into a spin, and she gave a moan of pleasure as his arms slid round her and he pulled her hard against his powerful frame.

'I want you.' He murmured the words against her lips, his mouth hot and demanding. 'I want you naked, right now.'

Her tummy tumbling, Holly gasped as he lifted her easily and carried her through to the gorgeous bedroom. The French doors remained open and she could hear the faint rush of the sea as he laid her down on the four-poster bed.

Would he notice that her boobs had grown and that her stomach was now slightly rounded? Holly squirmed slightly against the sheets and he kissed her again, using his skill and experience to drive away her inhibitions.

When he slid a hand over her stomach she tensed, and when his mouth trailed down her body she moaned and arched against him, unable to resist what he did to her.

And he did it over and over again, until she finally floated back down to earth, stunned and disconnected and with no clue as to how much time had passed.

Casper shifted above her, fire and heat flickering in his molten dark eyes as his satisfied gaze swept her flushed cheeks. 'I've *never* wanted a woman as much as I want you.'

Heart thudding, Holly gazed up at him. 'I love you.' The confession was torn from her in that moment of vulnerability, and she wrapped her arms round him and buried her face in his neck, breathing in the scent of virile male. 'I love you, Cas. I love you.'

And it was true, she realised helplessly. She did love him.

He was complicated, and he'd hurt her, but somewhere along the way she'd stopped trying to make their relationship work for the sake of the baby, and had started to fall in love.

Or perhaps it had always been there. From that first moment they'd met at the rugby match. Certainly there'd been *something*. How else could you explain the fact that she'd shared an intimacy with him she'd never shared with any other man?

Shocked by her own revelation, it took her a moment to realise that Casper had made no response.

He hadn't spoken and he hadn't moved.

It was as if her words had turned him to stone.

And then he rolled out of the affectionate circle of her arms and onto his back.

The honesty of her confession somehow made his sudden withdrawal all the more shocking. Wracked by a sense of isolation and rejection, Holly instinctively snuggled against him, but his tension was unmistakeable.

'Don't ever say that to me, Holly. Don't ever confuse great sex with love.'

'I'm not confused. I know what I feel. And I don't expect you to say it back, but that doesn't mean I can't say it to you.' Tentatively, she slid her arm over the flat, muscular plains of his stomach. 'I love you. And you don't have to be afraid of that.'

He muttered something under his breath and then shook her off and sprang off of bed. '"I love you" has to be the most overused phrase in the English language. So overused that it's lost its meaning.'

Holly crumpled as she watched her gift devalued in a single stroke. 'It hasn't lost its meaning to me.'

'No?' His eyes hard, he thrust his arms into a robe. 'Usually when people say "I love you" they mean something else. They mean, "you're great in bed", or perhaps, "I love the fact that you're rich and you can show me a good time". For you it's probably, "I love the fact that you were prepared to take on my baby".'

Holly flinched as though he'd slapped her. 'How can you say that?' Her voice cracked. 'Even after this time we've spent together, you still don't know me, do you? I'm trying to do what's best for our child, and you're being needlessly cruel—'

'Honest.'

'I've never said those words to anyone in my life before, and you just threw them back in my face.' The breath trapped in her throat, she watched him. 'Just so that there is no mis-understanding, let me tell you what "I love you" means to me. It means that I care more about your happiness than my own. And I care *all the time*, not just when we're having great sex. "I love you" means ignoring the pain you inflict every time you accuse me of lying, because I *know* you've been hurt yourself even though you won't talk to me about it. It means being patient and trying to accept that you find it hard to share your thoughts and feelings with me. And it's because I love you that I'm still standing here, swallowing my pride and trying to make this work, even when you hurt me on purpose.'

There was a long, deathly silence and then he lifted his hands, pressed his fingers to his temples and inhaled deeply. 'If that's really what you feel, then I'm sorry,' he said hoarsely, and his voice was strangely thickened. 'I can't give you anything back. I don't have that capacity any more.'

Without waiting for her response, he strode out of the bedroom, leaving her alone.

CHAPTER EIGHT

As THE door slammed shut between them, Holly flopped back onto the pillows, emotionally shattered.

How had such a perfect evening ended so badly?

Why should her simple declaration of love have had such a dramatic effect on his mood?

She thought back to his dismissive comments about fairy stories, love and happy endings.

Yes, he'd lost his fiancée, but even extreme grief shouldn't lead to that degree of cynicism should it?

And what had he meant when he said he *couldn't* love?

Was he saying that he believed a person could only love once in their lives?

Was that what was going on in his head?

Or was he saying that he couldn't love *her?*

Frustrated and desperately upset, Holly slipped out of bed, slipped her arms into a silk robe and walked across the bedroom. She stood for a moment with her hand on the door, wanting to follow him and yet afraid of further rejection.

Her hand dropped to her side and she stared at the door, her head a whirlpool of indecision.

She wanted him to talk, and yet she was afraid of hearing what he had to say.

She didn't want to hear that loving and losing another woman had prevented him ever loving again.

Because that would mean that there was no hope for them.

And yet not talking about it wasn't going to change things, was it?

Hoping she was doing the right thing, Holly slowly opened the door, realising that she had no idea where he'd gone.

What if he'd left the *palazzo*?

And then she saw a chink of light under the door to the library that they'd been shown when they'd arrived earlier.

Taking a deep breath, she tapped lightly on the door and opened it.

Casper stood with his back to her, staring out of the window.

Holly closed the door carefully. 'Please don't walk away from me,' she said quietly. 'If we need to have a difficult conversation, then let's have it. But don't avoid it. We don't stand any chance if you don't talk to me.' She knew from the sudden tension in his shoulders that he'd heard her, but it seemed like ages before he responded.

'I can't give you what you want, Holly. Love wasn't part of our deal.'

'Stop talking about it as a deal!' She stared at his back helplessly. 'Could you *please* at least look at me? This is hard enough without being able to see your face.'

He turned and she froze in shock, because his handsome face looked as though it had been chiselled from white marble. His eyes were blank of expression and yet the depth of his pain was evident in the very stillness of his body.

'Talk to me, Cas.' Forgetting her own misery, she walked across to him. 'Why can't you love? Is it because you lost Antonia? Is that it? Is this still about your grief?' And then she saw something in his face—a hardness—and everything fell into place. His comments. His beliefs. His *cynicism*.

Suddenly she just *knew*. 'Oh God—she did something dreadful to you, didn't she?'

'Holly—'

Ignoring his warning tone, she slid her hand into his larger one. 'All this time I've been assuming you were madly in love with her, and perhaps you were once.' Her eyes were on his rigid profile. 'But she let you down, didn't she? That's the reason you were so cynical about my motives. That's the reason you say you can't love. You don't *want* to let yourself love. Because you loved once before and she hurt you so badly. She did something, I know she did. *Tell* me about it.'

'Holly.' His voice thickened, and he turned on her. 'Just leave it.'

'No, I won't leave it.' She tightened her grip on his hand, refusing to let him withdraw. 'I want to know. I *deserve* to know.' Tears clogged her throat. *'What did she do?'*

A muscle worked in his lean jaw, and he stared at her, his eyes empty of emotion. 'She was sleeping with my brother.'

His revelation was so unexpected that Holly just stared at him. 'Oh, dear God.'

He gave a twisted smile and looked at her, his eyes strangely blank of emotion. 'Shall I tell you what Antonia meant when she said "I love you"? She meant that she loved the glitter and glamour of royal life. All the high-profile stuff. Only in those days I was working flat out in a commercial role. I didn't do many public engagements. I never expected to be the ruling prince. I didn't even want it. But Antonia did. For her, "I love you" meant "I love what you can do for my lifestyle", and once she found someone who could do more for her she transferred her "love" to them. The life my brother offered her was just too tempting.'

'I'm so sorry.'

'Don't be. I was naïve.' He removed his hand from hers. 'I was young enough and arrogant enough not to question her notion of love. I thought she cared about me and that what we shared was real.'

'The accident.'

Casper drew in a breath. 'We were on a skiing trip, Antonia and I. My brother joined us unexpectedly, and that was when I realised what was going on. Stupidly I confronted both of them, right there, at the top of the mountain where the helicopter had dropped us. My brother skied off and she followed.' He was silent for a moment. 'I went after them but I was quite a way behind. They caught the full force of the avalanche. There was nothing I could do. I was swept into a tree and knocked unconscious.'

'Did you tell anyone?' Her voice was soft. 'When you recovered, did you tell anyone the truth?'

'The country was in a state of crisis—defiling my brother's memory would have achieved nothing.'

'Forget about your country—what about *you*?'

'I couldn't forget about my country. I had a responsibility to the people.'

Holly swallowed down the lump in her throat. 'So you just buried it inside and carried on.'

'Of course.'

'And the only way to cope with so much emotion was to block it out.' Impulsively she slid her arms around his waist. 'Now I understand why you don't believe in love. But that wasn't love, Cas. She didn't love you.'

He closed his hands over her shoulders and gently but firmly prised her away from him. 'Close your book of fairy tales, Holly.' His voice was rough. 'The fact that you know the truth doesn't change anything.'

'It changes it for me.'

'Then you're deluding yourself.' His tone was harsh. 'Inside that dreamy head of yours, you're telling yourself that I'll fall in love with you. And that is never going to happen.'

She ignored the shaft of pain. 'Because you're afraid of being hurt again?'

'After the accident I switched off my emotions because that was the only way of getting through each day. I didn't want to feel. I couldn't afford to feel. How could I fulfil my responsibilities if I was wallowing in my personal grief?'

'So you shut it down, but that doesn't mean—'

'Don't do this!' With a soft curse, he lifted her face to his and forced her to meet his gaze. 'I'm not capable of feeling. And I'm not capable of love. I don't want love to be part of my life. We share great sex. Be grateful for that.'

That bleak confession made her heart stumble, and her voice was barely a whisper in the dimly lit room as she voiced the question that had been worrying her since the day she'd discovered she was pregnant. 'If you really can't love me, then I'll try and accept that. But I have to ask you one thing, Casper.' She was so terrified of the answer that she almost couldn't bear to ask the question. But she *had* to ask it. 'Do you think you can love our baby?'

His gaze held hers for a long moment and then his hands dropped to his side. 'I don't know,' he said hoarsely. 'I honestly don't know.'

Her hopes crashed into a million pieces.

'Don't say that to me, Cas.'

'You wanted the truth. I'm giving you the truth.'

And this time it was Holly who walked out of the room and closed the door between them.

'I'm worried about her, Your Highness. She isn't eating properly and she cancelled an engagement this afternoon.'

Emilio's normally impassive features were creased with worry. 'That isn't like her. I thought you ought to know.'

Casper glanced up from the pile of official papers on his desk. 'I expect she's tired.' Holly had been asleep when he'd finally joined her in the bed the previous night. *Or had she been pretending?* He frowned, wondering why that thought hadn't occurred to him before. 'And pregnant women are often faddy in their eating.'

'The princess isn't faddy, sir.' Emilio acted as though his feet had been welded to the spot. 'She loves her food. Even hot-tempered Pietro didn't have a single tantrum when he was cooking for her. Since you came back from Rome two weeks ago, she has eaten next to nothing. And she's stopped singing.'

Casper slowly and carefully put down the draft proposal he was reading.

She'd also stopped smiling, talking and cuddling him.

Since that night in Rome, Holly had behaved with a polite formality that was totally at odds with her outgoing personality. She answered his questions, but she asked none of her own, and she was invariably in bed asleep by the time he joined her.

She was dragging herself around like a wounded animal trying to find a place to die, and Casper gritted his teeth.

He had no reason to feel guilty.

And it should be a matter of indifference to him that his Head of Security clearly suspected that he had something to do with Holly's current level of distress. 'You are responsible for her physical well-being, not her emotional health.' His tone cool, Casper closed the file on his desk. 'It isn't your concern.'

'The princess was extremely kind to me when Tomasso was ill.' Emilio stood there, looking as though a hurricane wouldn't dislodge him. 'I want to make sure nothing is wrong. Two days ago when she opened the new primary school she just picked at her food, and yesterday when lunch was sent up to the apartment it came back untouched. Shall I ask her staff to call the doctor?'

'She doesn't need the doctor.' Casper pushed back his chair violently and stood up. 'I'll talk to her.'

'I think she needs a doctor.' In response to the sardonic lift of Casper's eyebrows, Emilio coloured. 'It's just that, if there is something upsetting her, she might need to talk to someone.'

'*Talk* to someone?' Casper looked at him with naked incredulity. 'Emilio, since when did a hardened ex-special forces soldier advocate talking therapy?'

Emilio didn't back down. 'Holly likes to talk, Your Highness.'

'I had noticed.'

But he wasn't talking to her, was he? Casper lifted a hand and rubbed his fingers over his forehead. 'I'll talk to her, Emilio. Thank you for bringing it to my attention.'

Still Emilio didn't move. 'She might prefer to talk to someone outside. Someone who isn't close to her.'

'You think she won't want to talk to me?'

'You can be intimidating, sir. And you're very—blunt. Holly is very optimistic and romantic.'

Not any more. *He was fairly sure he'd killed both those traits.*

Reflecting on that fact, Casper sucked in a breath. 'I can't promise romantic, but I will make sure I'm approachable.'

'May I say one more thing, sir?'

'Can I stop you?'

Ignoring the irony in the prince's tone, Emilio ploughed on. 'I have been by your side since you were thirteen years old. Holly—Her Royal Highness,' he corrected himself hastily, 'Isn't like any of the women you've been with before. She's genuine.'

Genuine? Casper shook his head, not sure whether to be relieved that she'd done such a good PR job on his staff, or exasperated that everyone just took her at face value. They saw nothing beyond the pretty smile and the chatty personality. Apparently it hadn't occurred to a single other person that this baby might not be his. That genuine, kind Holly Phillips might have another side to her.

That people and relationships were not always the way they appeared.

He wondered whether his loyal Head of Security had known Antonia had been sleeping with his brother.

'Thank you, Emilio. I'll deal with it.'

'Will you still be attending the fundraising dinner, sir?'

Casper frowned. 'Yes, of course.'

'The car will be ready at seven-thirty, sir.'

'One question, Emilio.' Casper lifted a hand and the bodyguard stopped. 'Which engagement did she cancel?'

Emilio met his gaze. 'The opening of a new family centre for children from split families, sir. It was an initiative designed to give lone parents support and children the opportunity to spend time with male role-models.' He hesitated and then bowed. 'I'll arrange the car for later.'

Casper stood still for a moment.

Then he cursed long and fluently, cast a frustrated glance at the volume of work on his desk, and turned his back on it and strode through the private apartments looking for Holly.

Holly lay on the bed with her head under the pillow.

She had to get up.

She had things to do. Responsibilities.

But her mind was so exhausted with thinking and worrying that she couldn't move.

'Holly.'

The sound of Casper's voice made her curl the pillow over her head. She didn't want him to see that she'd been crying.

She didn't want to see him at all. 'Go away. I'm tired. I'm having a sleep.'

'We have to talk.'

She curled up like a foetus. 'I'm still trying to get over the last talk we had.'

She heard the strong tread of his footsteps, and then the pillow was firmly prised from the tight ball of her fists. 'You're going to suffocate yourself.'

Holly kept her face turned away from him. 'I think better under the pillow.'

The pillow landed on the floor with a soft thud, and then she felt his hands curve around her and he lifted her into a sitting position. 'I want to look at you when I talk to you.' His fingers lifted her chin and his eyes narrowed. '*Dio*, have you been crying?'

'No, my face always looks like a tomato.' Mortified, she jerked her chin away from his fingers. 'Just go away, Casper.'

But he didn't move.

'The staff tell me you're not eating. They're worried about you.'

'That's kind of them.' Holly rubbed her hands over her arms. 'But I don't fancy anything to eat.'

'You cancelled your engagement this afternoon.'

'I really am sorry about that.' She wished he wouldn't sit so close to her. *She couldn't concentrate when he was this close*. 'But the subject was a bit—painful. I just couldn't face it. I will go, I promise. The visit is going to be rearranged. Just not this week.' Why was it that she just wanted to fling her arms around his neck and sob?

Terrified that she'd give in to the impulse, she wriggled off the bed and walked over to the glass doors that were open onto the balcony.

A breeze played with the filmy curtains, and beyond the

profusion of plants she could see sunlight glistening on the surface of a perfect blue sea.

Although it was only early April, it promised to be a warm day.

And she'd never felt more miserable in her life.

'Forget the visit.' Casper gave a soft curse and strode across to her, pulling her into his arms. 'Enough, Holly.' His voice was rough. 'This is about Rome, isn't it? We've been dancing round the issue for two weeks. Perhaps I was a little too blunt.'

'You were honest.' She stood rigid in his arms, trying to ignore the excitement that fluttered to life in her tummy.

She didn't want to respond.

'You're making yourself ill.'

'It's just hard, that's all.' Holly tried to pull away from him but he held her firmly. 'Normally when I have a problem I talk it through and that's how I deal with things.'

He cupped her face, his eyes holding hers. 'Then talk it through.'

'You make it sound so simple. But who am I supposed to talk to, Casper?' Her voice was a whisper. 'It's all private stuff, isn't it? I can just imagine what some of the more unscrupulous staff would do with a story like that.'

His eyes narrowed. 'You're learning about the media.'

'Yes, well, I've had some experience now.' She was desperately aware of him—of the hardness of his thighs pressing against hers, of the strength of his arms as he held her firmly.

'This is your chance to get your revenge.'

'You really ought to get to know me, instead of just turning me into some stereotypical gold digger. I don't want revenge, Casper. I don't want to hurt you. I just want you to love our baby.' And her. She wanted him to love her. 'And the fact that you can't…' The dilemma started to swirl in her head again. 'I don't know what to do.'

'You've lost weight.' His hands slid slowly down her arms and his mouth tightened. 'You can start by eating.'

'I'm not hungry.'

'Then you should be thinking about the baby.'

It was like pulling the pin out of a hand grenade.

Erupting with a violence that was new to her, Holly lifted a hand and slapped him hard. 'How *dare* you tell me I should be thinking about the baby? I think of nothing else!' Sobbing with fury and outrage, she backed away from him, his stunned expression blurring as tears pricked her eyes. 'From the moment I discovered I was pregnant the baby is the *only* thing I've been thinking of. When you turned up at the flat, that day you were *horrid* to me, I spent two weeks going round and round in circles trying to work out what to do for the best, but I decided that, as this is your baby, marrying you was the right thing to do. Even when you told me that you believe you're infertile I didn't panic, because I know it isn't true and sooner or later you're going to know that too. Then you told me that you couldn't ever love me and that *hurt*—' Her voice cracked. 'Yes, it hurt, but I made myself accept it because I kept reminding myself that it isn't me that matters. But when you said you didn't know if you could love our baby—'

'Holly.' His voice was tight. 'You have to calm down—'

'Don't tell me to calm down! Antonia did a dreadful thing to you. Really dreadful. But that isn't our baby's fault. And now I don't know what to do.' She paced the floor, so agitated that she couldn't keep still. 'What sort of a mother would I be if I stayed with a man who can't love his own child? I always thought that the only thing that mattered was to have a father. But is it worse to grow up with a father who doesn't love you? I don't know, and maybe I've done the wrong thing by marrying you, maybe I am a bad mother, but don't *ever* accuse me of not thinking about our baby!'

Casper muttered something in Italian and ran a hand over the back of his neck, tension visible in every angle of his powerful frame. 'I did *not* say that you were a bad mother.'

'But you implied it.'

'Enough!' It was a command, and Holly stilled, her legs trembling so much that she was almost relieved when he strode towards her and scooped her into his arms.

'I hate you,' she whispered, and then she burst into tears and buried her face in his shoulder.

'*Dio*, you have to stop this, you're making yourself ill. Ssh.' He laid her gently on the bed and then lay down next to her and pulled her into his arms, ignoring her attempts to resist. 'Calm down.' He stroked her hair away from her face but Holly couldn't stop crying.

'I'm sorry I hit you. I'm sorry.' Her breath was coming in jerks. 'I've never hit anyone in my life before. It's just that I so badly want you to love the baby. I *need* you to love it, Cas.' She covered her face with her hands. 'You don't know what it's like to have a father that doesn't care. It makes you feel worthless. If your own father doesn't love you, why should anyone else?'

He gave a soft curse, rolled her onto her back and lowered his body onto hers.

Then he gently removed her hands and wiped her face with the edge of the sheet.

'Hush.'

Still crying, she pushed at his powerful chest. 'Cas, don't—' But her protest was cut off by the demands of his mouth, and within seconds she could no longer remember why she hadn't wanted him to kiss her.

The explosion of sexual excitement anaesthetised the turmoil in her brain and she kissed him back, her body responding to his.

Only when she was soft and compliant did Casper finally lift his head.

'Don't use sex like this,' she moaned, and he gave a grim smile.

'I was trying to stop you crying. Now it is my turn to talk,' he said softly. 'And you're not going to interrupt.' He wiped her damp cheeks with a sweep of his thumb. 'I won't make you false promises of love. I can't do that, and it wouldn't be fair to you because I will not lie. But I do promise you this.' His dark eyes locked with hers, demanding her attention. 'I promise that I will be a good father to the baby. I promise that I will not walk off and leave the child, as your father did to you. I promise that I will do everything in my power to make sure that the child grows up feeling secure and valued. I accepted responsibility for the child and I intend to fulfil that responsibility to the best of my ability.'

Numb, sodden with misery, Holly stared up at him. It wasn't what she wanted, but it was a start. And, if he was prepared to do that for a child that he didn't believe was his, perhaps once he discovered that he was the baby's father then...

He'd coped with hurt by turning off his emotions. Maybe nothing could switch them back on again.

Her natural optimism flickered to life.

But she could hope.

'Your favourite lunch, Your Highness. *Pollo alla limone*.'

'Yum.' Holly put down the letter she was writing. 'Pietro, you have no idea how grateful I am that you decided to leave England and work here for a while. The whole of the palace must be rejoicing. Not that the other chefs weren't brilliant, of course,' she said hastily, and Pietro smiled as he placed a simple green salad next to the chicken.

'I'm not cooking for the rest of the palace, madam. Just for you. Those were the prince's orders.'

'Really? I didn't know that.' Thinking of all the other thoughtful gestures the prince had made since that terrible afternoon when she'd hit him, something softened inside her. 'He brought you all the way over here, for *me?*'

'His Royal Highness is most concerned about your comfort and happiness. But so are we all. You and the *bambino.* You say jump, we say "off which cliff?"' Pietro beamed as he lifted a jug. 'Sicilian lemonade?'

'Don't even bother asking. You know I'm addicted.' Smiling, Holly held out her glass to be filled. 'So, are you happy here?'

'*Si,* because to see you blooming with health gives me satisfaction. And when the baby comes no one will prepare his food except me! I have talked to the gardeners, and we are designing a special vegetable patch—all organic and grown in the Santallia sunshine.'

'Puréed Santallian carrot—' Taking a mouthful of chicken, Holly almost choked as she noticed Casper standing in the doorway.

Sunlight glinted off his dark hair, and he looked so outrageously handsome that her heart dropped.

Why did she have to feel like this?

It was no wonder she struggled to keep a degree of emotional distance when he had such a powerful effect on her.

Right from that very first day at the rugby, she'd failed to hold herself back.

Even now, when she knew he had the ability to hurt her and her child, she was willing to risk it all.

She swallowed the lump of food in her mouth and put down her fork. 'I—I didn't know you were joining me for lunch. Here—' she pushed her plate towards him '—Pietro always cooks for the five thousand—we can share.'

'No, madam!' Appalled, Pietro clasped his hands in front of him and then remembered himself and bowed stiffly. 'I can bring more from the kitchen.'

'*Grazie.*' Casper gave Pietro a rare smile and sat down opposite Holly, his eyes on the pile of envelopes. 'You've been busy.'

'I'm replying to all these children who are sending me pictures and letters. There are hundreds. And look, Cas.' Relieved for an excuse to focus on something other than the way he made her feel, Holly put down her fork and reached for a pink envelope. 'A little girl sent me this soft toy she made. Isn't it sweet?'

Casper's brows rose as he stared at the object. 'What is it supposed to be?'

'Well, it's…' Holly studied the pink fluffy wedge closely and then frowned. 'I thought it might be a pig, or possibly a sheep. I'm not absolutely sure,' she conceded, 'But I love it. She's only six. Don't you think it's brilliant?'

'So you are writing to thank her for sending you a something?' Casper stretched his legs out, his eyes amused. 'That is one letter I would like to read.'

'I'll think of something to say.' Holly put the fluffy object away carefully. 'People are so kind. And talking of kind…' She bit her lip and looked up at him. 'Thank you for arranging for Pietro to come here. And for flying Nicky out for a week. That was so thoughtful.'

'I thought you needed someone to talk to. And she was very loyal to you when you were in trouble.'

'Is that why you gave her that beautiful bracelet? She loved it. And we had such a good time at the beach. Thank you.'

He seemed about to say something in response, but at that moment several staff appeared with lunch.

Pietro served the prince with a flourish. 'If there is anything else, please call,' he murmured and then retreated, leaving them alone.

Casper glanced at Holly. 'Eat,' he drawled, 'Or Pietro will resign.'

Holly smiled, very conscious of his eyes on her. 'I'd be the size of a small-tower block if I ate everything Pietro gave me.'

'Does that explain why the palace cats are putting on weight?'

Holly picked up her fork again. 'I *am* eating.'

'I know. The doctor is very happy with your health, including your weight gain.'

Her heart fluttered. 'You asked him?'

Their eyes clashed. 'I care, Holly.'

She believed him. He'd demonstrated that over and over again. But it was impossible to forget the words he'd spoken in Rome. And she couldn't stop asking herself whether caring was going to be enough. 'The nursery is finished.' Pushing the thought away, she gave a bright smile. 'The designer you suggested is brilliant. It looks gorgeous.'

'Good. I bought you a present.' He handed her a box. 'I hope you like it.'

Holly's hand shook as she took it from him. 'I don't need anything.'

'A present shouldn't be something you need. It should be wantonly extravagant.'

Holly flipped open the box and gasped. 'Well, it's certainly that!' Carefully she lifted the diamond bracelet from its velvet nest. 'It matches my necklace.'

He was trying to compensate for the fact that he didn't love her.

The thought almost choked her.

'*Now* what's wrong?' His voice rough, he laid his fork down.

'Nothing.' She fastened the bracelet around her wrist and gave him a brilliant smile. 'What could possibly be wrong?'

'You're holding back. For once there is plenty going on in your head that isn't coming out of your mouth, and that makes me uneasy.' After a moment's hesitation, he reached across the table to take her hand. 'You're still not yourself, Holly. I feel as though I can never quite reach you.'

'We're together every night.'

'Physically, yes. We have incredible sex and then you turn your back on me and say good night.'

Colour flaming in her cheeks, Holly studied the remains of the chicken on her plate.

She could feel the hot sunshine on the back of her neck, the whisper of a breeze playing with her hair and the blaze of heat in his eyes as he watched her.

'I'm trying to—we're different.' Staring miserably at the glittering diamonds, she wondered absently whether the extravagance of the gift was inversely related to his feelings for her. *The emptier his heart, the bigger the diamonds?* 'I'm very demonstrative by nature, and you're—not. All the worst moments in our relationship have been when I've shown my feelings. You back off. You shut down like a nuclear reactor detecting a leak. Nothing must escape.'

Casper frowned and his grip tightened on her hand. 'So you're protecting me?'

'No.' Finally she lifted her eyes and looked at him. 'I'm protecting myself.'

CHAPTER NINE

DETERMINED to keep busy, Holly threw herself into her public engagements and wrote as many personal replies as she could to the many letters and cards she received. She discovered that if she kept herself busy she didn't think so much and that was a good thing because her thoughts frightened her.

She didn't want to think what might happen if Casper didn't love their baby.

And, since that couldn't immediately be resolved, she pushed the thought away.

When the baby was born, she'd worry. Until then, she'd hope.

And in the meantime she fussed in the nursery, as if being born into perfect surroundings might somehow compensate for deficiencies in other areas of the baby's life.

She was sitting in the hand-carved rocking chair, reading a book about childbirth one morning, when one of the palace staff told her she had a personal visitor.

Not expecting anyone, Holly put the book down and walked through to the beautiful living-room with the windows overlooking the sparkling Mediterranean.

Eddie stood there, looking awkward and out of place.

'Eddie?' Shocked to see him, Holly walked quickly across the room. 'What are you doing here?'

'What sort of a question is that? We were friends once.'
He gave a twisted smile. 'Or can't you have friends now
you're a royal?'

'Of course I can have friends.' Holly blushed, feeling really
awkward and uncomfortable and not sure why. 'But obviously
I wasn't expecting to see you and—how are you?'

'OK. Doing well, actually. The job's turning out well.'

'Good. I'm pleased for you.' And she was, she realised,
picking over her feelings carefully. She wasn't angry with
him. If anything, she was grateful. If he hadn't broken their
engagement, she might well have married him, and that would
have been the biggest mistake of her life—because she knew
now that she didn't love him and she never had.

Loving Casper had taught her what love was, and it wasn't
what she'd felt for Eddie.

'I was owed some holiday.' Thrusting his hands into his
pockets, he walked over to the windows. 'I'm spending a
week in the Italian lakes, but I thought I'd call in here on the
way. Booked myself a room at the posh hotel on the beach.
Stunning view. Can't imagine Lake Como being any prettier
than this.' He took a deep breath, rubbed a hand over the back
of his neck and turned to face her. 'I came here to apologise,
actually. For going to the press. I— It was a rotten thing to do.'

'It's OK. You were upset.' Touched that he'd bothered to
apologise, Holly smiled. 'People do funny things when
they're upset.'

'I didn't mean to make things difficult for you.' Eddie
shrugged sheepishly. 'Well, I suppose I did. I was angry and
jealous and—' he cleared his throat '—I wasn't sure if you'd
want to see me to be honest. But I needed to say sorry. I've
been feeling guilty.'

'Please don't give it another thought.'

Eddie seemed relieved. 'It was jolly hard getting in to see

you. Layers and layers of security. It was that big fellow who fixed it for me.'

'Emilio?'

'That's him. The prince's henchman. Not that the prince needs him. From what I can gather, he can fire his own gun if the need arises. Is he treating you well?'

Holly thought about the diamonds and the long nights spent in sexual ecstasy. And she thought about the fact he didn't love her.

'He's treating me well.'

'Just thought I'd check.' Eddie gave a lopsided smile. 'In case you'd changed you mind and wanted to escape.' He waved a hand around their luxurious surroundings. 'I might not be able to offer you a palace, but—'

'I never wanted a palace, Eddie,' Holly said softly, resting a hand protectively over the baby. 'Family, being loved—those are the things that are important to me.'

'I was going to say I think I was a bit too ambitious for you, but then I realised how bloody stupid that sounds now that you're living with a prince in a palace!' He pulled a face. 'We weren't absolutely right together, were we?'

'No, we weren't,' Holly said honestly. 'And ambition has nothing to do with the reason I'm living here. Cas is my baby's father, Eddie. That's why I'm here.'

'To begin with I was so angry with you. I thought you'd tried to make a fool out of me—'

Holly frowned. 'I'm not like that.'

'I know you're not,' Eddie said, a bit too hastily. 'I hope the prince knows how lucky he is. Anyway, I ought to be going.'

'Already? Don't you want coffee or something?' Holly walked across to him and held out a hand in a gesture of conciliation. 'It was sweet of you to come and see me. I appreciate it. And sweet of you to apologise.'

He hesitated and then took her hand. 'I just wanted to check you're OK. If you ever need anything…'

'She has everything she needs.' A harsh voice came from behind them, and Holly turned to see Casper standing in the doorway, his eyes glittering like shards of ice.

Visibly nervous, Eddie gave a slight bow. 'Your Highness. I— Well, I just wanted to see Holly—say hello—you know how it is. I was just leaving.'

Casper's threatening gaze didn't shift from his face. 'I'll show you out.'

Shocked and more than a little embarrassed by Casper's rudeness, Holly gave Eddie a hug to make up for it. 'Thank you for looking me up.'

Eddie hugged her back awkwardly, one eye on the prince. 'Good to see you looking so well. Bye, Holly.' He left the living room, and moments later Casper strode back into the room, his eyes simmering black with anger.

'I allow you a great deal of freedom,' he said savagely, 'But I do not expect you to entertain your lover in our living room.'

'That's ridiculous.' Holly watched him unravel with appalled disbelief. 'He is *not* my lover. And I don't understand why you're being possessive.'

He didn't care about her, did he?

He didn't want her love.

'But he *was* your lover!' A thunderous expression on his face, Casper prowled across the living room, tension emanating from every bit of his powerful frame. 'And yes, I'm possessive! When I find the father of your baby in my living room, holding your hand, I'm possessive!'

Something snapped inside Holly.

'I never had sex with Eddie! I have never slept with anyone except you!' Consumed by an anger she didn't know she could feel, Holly threw the words at him. 'All you ever say is *your* baby, but it's *our* baby, Casper. *This is your baby too.* And I'm sick of tiptoeing round the issue.'

His voice strangely thickened, Casper faced her down. 'Don't ever, *ever* touch another man!'

'Why? I *like* hugging, and you don't want me hugging you!' Flinging the words at him like bricks, Holly took a step backwards, a hand over her stomach. 'I can't live like this any more. I can't live in this—this—emotional desert! I'm afraid to touch you in case you back away, and I'm afraid to speak in case I say the wrong thing. I've tried *so hard* to do everything right. I know this marriage wasn't what you wanted, but I've done my best. I've worked and worked, and I've been *loyal.* I haven't once talked about you to anyone, not even when you pushed me away and I was so lonely I wanted to die! But not once, in all that time, have I ever given you reason not to trust me.'

A muscle flickered in his jaw. 'It isn't a question of trust.'

'Of course it is!' Her voice was high-pitched and unlike her usual tone. 'I forgave you for what you thought about me at the beginning of our relationship because I was honest enough to admit that I didn't exactly behave like a virgin, even though that's what I was. I've made allowances for the fact that Antonia hurt you so badly, and I've made allowances for the fact that your position as ruling prince meant you weren't allowed to grieve. But when have you *ever* made allowances for me? Never. Not once have you given me the benefit of the doubt. *Not once.*' Her heart was racing and she felt suddenly light-headed.

Casper inhaled sharply. 'Holly—'

'*Don't look at me as if I've lost it!* I am *not* hysterical. In fact, this is probably the sanest moment I've had since I've met you. I've always assumed that you act the way you do because of Antonia, but I'm starting to think it has more to do with your bloody ego!'

'I've never heard you swear before.'

'Yes, well, our relationship has been full of firsts. First sex, first swearing, first slap around the face—' Feeling the baby kick, Holly placed a hand on her bump and rubbed gently. 'You know what I think, Cas? I don't think this has anything to do with Antonia. I think it's more to do with your macho, alpha, king of the world, dominant—' she waved a hand, searching for more adjectives '—*man* thing. You couldn't bear the thought that I'd slept with another man, and the really ridiculous, crazy thing is *I haven't*!'

'You were engaged to him.'

'But I didn't have sex with him! That's the main reason he dumped me, because I was too shy to take my clothes off!' She glared at him, silencing his next remark with a warning glance. 'And *don't* ask me what happened when I met you, because I still haven't worked that one out. You have a way of undressing a woman that James Bond would envy.'

'You were devastated when you broke up with him.'

'Obviously not *that* devastated or I wouldn't have been having crazy, abandoned sex on a table with you the next day.' A hysterical laugh escaped from her throat. 'Just because you're incapable of indulging in a relationship that doesn't include sex, it doesn't mean I'm the same. Now get out, and stay away from me until you've learned how to be human.'

In the grip of a savage rage, Casper strode through his private rooms and slammed the door of his study.

He'd lost his temper with a pregnant woman.

What had he been thinking?

But he knew the answer to that. He hadn't been thinking at all.

From the moment he'd walked into the living room and seen Eddie standing there holding Holly's hand, his brain had been engulfed in a fiery fog of red-hot jealousy.

Never before had he felt the overwhelming urge to wipe another person from the face of the earth, but he had today.

The thought that Eddie had been near her.

He felt physically sick, his forehead damp and his palms sweating.

He needed to apologise to Holly, but first he needed to make sure that Eddie didn't set foot in her life again.

Not pausing to question the sense of his actions, he ordered his driver to take him to the hotel where Eddie was staying. Ignoring the amazed looks of the hotel reception-staff as they gave him the room number he wanted, Casper dismissed his security guards and then took the stairs two at a time.

Outside the room, he took a deep breath.

He was *not* going to kill him.

Having forced that thought into his head, he hammered on the door.

Eddie pulled it open and the colour drained from his face. 'Your Highness—this is—'

'Why did you break the engagement?' Casper slammed the door shut behind him, guaranteeing their privacy.

Eddie's mouth worked like a fish, and then he gave a slight smile and a shrug, his ego reasserting itself. 'Man to man? Actually I met a stunning blonde. She had amazing—you know.' He gestured with his hands and Casper gritted his teeth and forced himself to ask the question he'd come to ask.

'Did you sleep with Holly?' His voice was thickened, and Eddie gave a confident smile and a knowing wink.

'God, yes—she was bloody insatiable.'

Forgetting his promise to himself, Casper punched the other man hard in the jaw and Eddie staggered backwards, clutching his face.

'God, you've broken my jaw—I'll have you for this!'

'Go ahead.' Casper hauled the man to his feet by the front

of his shirt, ignoring the tearing sound as the fabric gave way. 'So you had sex with Holly, and then you dumped her. Is that what you expect me to believe?'

Eddie touched his jaw gingerly. 'Some girls you have sex with, some girls you marry, you know what I mean?' Fear flickered in his eyes as he registered Casper's expression. 'Still, money changes a person. I'm sure she's changed since she's married you, Your Highness.'

'Are you? I think Holly is the same girl she's always been.' His tone flat, Casper released the other man, shaking him off like a bug from a leaf.

Eddie spluttered with relief and backed away, his hand on his jaw, and then his chest. 'You ripped my shirt.'

'You're lucky I stopped at your shirt.'

'Do you know how much I'm going to get for this story?' Eddie's face was scarlet with rage and Casper shot him a contemptuous glance.

'So it *was* you who sold the story to the paper the first time.'

'Is that what Holly told you?'

'*Don't* call her Holly. To you, it's Her Royal Highness.' Casper flexed his long fingers and had the satisfaction of seeing Eddie take another step backwards. 'And if you *ever* mention the princess's name again, the next thing I rip will be your throat.'

'I thought princes were supposed to be civilised,' Eddie squeaked from his position of safety, and Casper gave a slow, dangerous smile as he strode towards the door.

'I never did believe in fairy stories.'

'I'll be fine, Emilio, honestly. I just feel like some sea air, and The Dowager Cottage is so pretty, right on the sand. It reminds me of the night before my wedding.' *When she'd still been full of hope.*

Holly's face ached from the effort of smiling, and she stuffed a few items into a large canvas bag, as if a day on the beach was just what she wanted, but Emilio didn't look convinced.

'I will call His Highness and—'

'No, don't do that.' Holly interrupted him quickly, wincing as the baby kicked her hard. 'I just want to be on my own for a bit.'

And she didn't want to be in the palace when Casper eventually returned from wherever it was he'd stalked off to.

She just couldn't stand yet another confrontation.

And she had no idea what they were going to do about their marriage. Could they really limp along like this with just her love and hot sex to hold them together?

Was it enough?

Her head started to throb again and she made a conscious effort to switch off her thoughts for the baby's sake, wondering whether the tension was the reason he was kicking so violently.

For the baby's sake, she needed to try and relax.

Without further question, Emilio summoned her driver, and once she arrived at The Dowager Cottage Holly kicked off her shoes and made a conscious effort to unwind. 'I'm just going to sit on the beach for a bit.' She smiled at the man who had become a friend. 'Thanks, Emilio.'

'Pietro made you this, madam.' He handed her a small bag. 'Just a few of your favourite snacks.'

'He is such a sweetie.' Choked by the warmth that they'd showed her, she suddenly rose on tiptoe to kiss Emilio. 'And so are you,' she said huskily, her lips brushing his cheek. 'You've been *so* kind to me all the way through this. Thank you.'

Emilio cleared his throat. 'You are a very special person, madam.'

'I'm a waitress,' Holly reminded him with a dry tone, but Emilio shook his head.

'No.' His voice was soft. 'You're a princess. In every sense that matters.'

Holly blinked several times and suddenly found that she had a lump in her throat. She was so touched by his words that for a moment she couldn't reply.

She *could* be happy with her life, she told herself. She had friends.

'Well, let's hope that's one kiss that the paparazzi didn't manage to catch on camera.' Lightening the atmosphere with a cheeky wink, she walked onto the sand.

'I'll be right here, madam,' Emilio called after her, adjusting the tiny radio he wore in his ear. 'You know how to call me.'

'Thanks. But no one has access to this beach. I'll be fine. Go inside and relax. It's too hot to stand out here.'

Her pale-blue sun dress swinging around her bare calves, Holly walked to the furthest end of the beautiful curving beach and plopped herself down on the sand.

For a while she just stared out to sea. Then she opened the bag Pietro had sent, but discovered she wasn't hungry.

Finally she opened her book.

'You're holding that book upside down. And you should be wearing a hat.' Casper stood there, tall and powerful, the width of his shoulders shading her from the sun. 'You'll burn.'

Holly dropped the book onto the sand. 'Please go away. I want to be alone.' *What she didn't want was to feel this immediate rush of pleasure that always filled her whenever he was near.*

'You *hate* being on your own,' he responded instantly. 'You are the most sociable person I have ever met.'

Holly brushed the sand from the book, her fingers shaking. 'That depends on the company.'

His arrogant, dark head jerked back as though she'd hit him

again, but instead of retaliating he settled himself on the sand next to her, the unusual tension in his shoulders suggesting that he was less than sure of his welcome.

'You're *extremely* angry with me, and I can't blame you for that.' He studied her for a moment and then reached gently for her hand and curled her slender fingers into a fist. 'You can hit me again if you like.'

'It didn't make me feel any better.' She pulled her hand away from his, hating herself for feeling a thrill of excitement instead of indifference. 'And I'd be grateful if you'd stop looking at me like that.'

'How am I looking at you?'

'You're sizing up the situation so that you can decide which of your slick diplomatic skills are required to talk me round.'

'I wish it were that easy.' Casper lifted one broad shoulder in a resigned gesture. 'Unfortunately for me, I have no previous experience of handling a situation like this.'

'Which is?'

'Grovelling.' A gleam of self-mockery glinting in his sexy eyes, he reached for her hand again, this time locking it firmly in his. 'I was wrong about you. The baby is mine. I know that now.'

Holly closed her eyes tightly, swamped by a rush of emotions so powerful that she couldn't breathe.

He believed her. He trusted her.

Finally, he trusted her.

And then she realised that something wasn't quite right about his sudden confession and her eyes flew open. 'Wait a minute.' She snatched her hand away from his because she couldn't keep her mind focused when he was touching her. 'The last time I saw you, you were accusing me of having an affair with Eddie—when did you suddenly become rational?'

Dark streaks of colour highlighted his aristocratic bone

structure, and Casper spread his hands in a gesture of conciliation. 'I believe you, Holly. That's all that matters.'

'No.' Holly scrambled to her feet, knowing that she only stood a chance of thinking clearly if he wasn't within touching distance. 'No, it isn't. You went to the doctor, didn't you?'

A muscle flickered in his bronzed cheek. 'Yes.'

Holly wrapped her arms around her waist and gave a painful laugh. 'So you placed your trust in medical science, not me.'

'Holly…'

'So they've told you that you're capable of fathering a child. That's good. But it still doesn't tell you that this child is yours, does it?'

His stunning dark eyes narrowed warily, as if he sensed a trick question. 'I have no doubt that the baby is mine.' He drew in a long breath, his shimmering gaze fixed on her face, assessing her reaction. 'I have no doubt that you have been telling me the truth all along.'

'Really? What makes you so confident that I didn't have sex with the whole rugby team once I'd finished with you?' Her voice rising, Holly winced as the baby planted another kick against her ribs, and glared as Casper lifted a hand in what was obviously intended to be a conciliatory gesture.

'You're overreacting because you're pregnant. You're very hormonal and—'

'Hormonal? Don't patronise me! And anyway, if I'm hormonal, what's *your* excuse? You overreact all the time! You accuse me of having sex with just about everyone, even though it should have been perfectly obvious to you that I'd never been with a man before. You thought I was some scheming hussy doing some sort of—of—' she searched for an analogy '—paternity lottery. Trying to win first prize of a prince in the "most eligible daddy" contest.'

Casper rose to his feet, a tall, powerful figure, as imposing in casual clothes as he was in a dinner jacket. His mouth tightened and his lean, strong face was suddenly watchful. 'You have to agree I had reason to feel like that.'

'To begin with, maybe. But *not* once you knew me.' Dragging her eyes away from the hint of bronzed male skin at the neck of his shirt, Holly stooped and stuffed her few items back into her bag. She wasn't going to look at him. So, he was devastatingly handsome. So what? 'I loved you, Casper, and you threw it back at me because you're afraid.'

He inhaled sharply. 'I am not afraid. And you're stuffing sand in your bag along with the books.'

'I don't care about the sand! And you *are* afraid—you're so afraid you've shut yourself down so that you can't ever be hurt again.' Frustrated and upset, she emptied her bag and started again, this time shaking the sand onto the beach.

Casper stepped towards her, dark eyes glittering. 'I came here to apologise.'

Holly stared at him, wishing he wasn't so indecently handsome. *Wishing that she didn't still ache for him to touch her.* 'Then you definitely need more practice, because where I come from apologies usually contain the word sorry at least once.' With a violent movement, she hooked the bag onto her shoulder and reached for her hat, but he caught her arm and held her firmly.

'You are *not* walking away from me.'

'Watch me.' With her free hand, she jammed the hat onto her head and then gasped as he swung her into his arms. 'Put me down *right now*.'

'No.' Ignoring her protest and her wriggling, Casper walked purposefully to the end of the beach, took a narrow path without breaking stride and then lowered her onto soft white sand.

'You've probably put your back out,' Holly muttered, her

fingers curling over his warm, bronzed shoulders to steady herself. 'And it serves you right.'

'You don't weigh anything.'

Noticing their surroundings for the first time, Holly gave a soft gasp of shock, because she'd never seen anywhere quite as beautiful.

'I had no idea there was another beach here. It's stunning.'

'When we were children, my brother and I called it the secret beach.' His tone gruff, Casper spread the rug on the sand and gently eased the bag from her shoulders. 'We used to play here, knowing that no one could see us. It was probably the only real privacy we had in our childhood. We made camps, dens, we were pirates and smugglers, and—'

'All right—enough.' Emotion welling up inside her, Holly held up a hand, and Casper looked at her with exasperation.

'I thought talking was good.'

'*Not* when I'm angry with you.' Holly flopped onto the rug and shot him a despairing look. 'I'm so, *so* angry with you, and when you start talking like that I find it really hard to stay angry.'

Evidently clocking that up as a point in his favour, Casper joined her on the rug, his usual confidence apparently fully restored by her reluctant confession. 'You find it hard to be angry with me?' Gently, he pushed her onto her back and supported himself on one elbow as he looked down at her. 'You have forgiven me?'

'No.' She closed her eyes tightly so that she couldn't see his thick dark lashes and impossibly sexy eyes. But she could feel him looking at her. 'You've hurt me *really* badly.'

'*Sì*, I have. But now I am saying sorry. Open your eyes.'

'No. I don't want to look at you.'

'Open your eyes, *tesoro*.' His voice was so gentle that her eyes fluttered open, and she tumbled instantly into the depths of his dark eyes.

'Nothing you say is going to make any difference,' she muttered, and he gave a slow smile.

'I know that isn't true. You're always telling me that I should know who you are by now, and I think I do.' He lifted his hand and stroked her cheek gently. 'I know you are a very forgiving person.'

'Not that forgiving.' Her heart was pounding against her chest, but she refused to make it easy for him.

Lowering his head, Casper brought his mouth down on hers in a devastatingly gentle kiss that blew her mind. 'I am sorry, *angelo mio*. I am sorry for not believing that the baby was mine—for implying that you targeted me.'

Holly lay still, waiting, hoping, praying, *dying a little*— knowing that he was never going to say what she wanted to hear.

His eyes quizzical, Casper gently turned her face towards him. 'I'm apologising.'

'I know.'

He frowned. 'I'm saying sorry.'

'Yes.' His apparent conviction that he'd done what needed to be done made her want to hit him again and he gave an impatient sigh.

'Clearly I'm saying the wrong things, because you're lying there like a martyr burning at the stake. *Dio*, what is it that you want from me?' Without waiting for her answer, he lowered his mouth to hers and kissed her with devastating expertise.

Holly was immediately plunged into an erotic, sensual world that sucked her downwards. Struggling back to the surface, she gasped, 'I don't want to do this, Casper—'

'Yes, you do—this side of our relationship has always been good.' He eased his lean, powerful frame over hers, careful to support most of his weight on his elbows. 'Am I hurting the baby?'

'No, but I don't want you to—' She broke off as she saw his expression change. 'What? What's the matter?'

'The baby kicked me.' There was a strange note to his voice, and Holly felt her heart flip because she'd never seen Casper less than fully in control of every situation. He pulled away slightly and slid a bold but curious hand over the smooth curve of her abdomen. 'He kicked me really hard.'

'Good. Because quite frankly, if you weren't pinning me to the sand at this precise moment, I'd kick you myself for being so arrogant!' Holly glared at him but his face broke into a slow, sure smile of masculine superiority as he transferred his hand to the top of her thigh.

'No, you wouldn't. You're non-violent.'

'Funnily enough, *not* since I met you,' Holly gritted, and he gave a possessive smile.

'I bring out your passionate side, I know. And I love the way you're prepared to fight for my baby.'

'*Your* baby? So now you think you produced it all by yourself? Just because you've finally decided to acknowledge the truth—' Holly gasped as Casper shifted purposefully above her, amusement shimmering in his gorgeous dark eyes as his mouth hovered tantalisingly close to hers.

Tiny sparks of fire heated her pelvis, and her whole body was consumed by an overpowering hunger for this man.

Her mouth was dry, her heart was thundering in her chest, and she couldn't drag her eyes away from his beautiful mouth and the dangerous glitter in his eyes. 'Cas—you're squashing the baby!'

'I'm putting no weight on you at all,' he breathed, one sure, confident hand sliding under her summer dress and easing her thighs apart.

And then, with a slow smile that said everything about his intentions, he lowered his head. His mouth captured hers in a raw, demanding kiss just as his skilled fingers gently explored the moist warmth of their target, and Holly exploded with a hot, electrifying excitement that eradicated everything from her brain except pure wicked pleasure.

She ached, she throbbed, she was *desperate*, and when he slid a hand beneath her hips and lifted her she wound her legs around him in instinctive invitation, urging him on.

She'd become accustomed to the wild, uninhibited nature of their love-making. Right from the start the sexual chemistry had been so explosive that there had been times when it was hard to know which of them was the most out of control.

But this time felt different.

Casper surged into her quivering, receptive body and then paused, his breathing ragged as he scanned her flushed cheeks. 'Am I hurting you?'

'No.' Not in the way he meant.

Holly closed her eyes tightly, moaning as he eased himself deeper, every thought driven from her head by the silken strength of him inside her.

She'd never known him so careful, and yet there was something about the slow, deliberate thrusts that were shockingly erotic.

She was no longer aware of the warmth of the sun or the sounds of the sea, because everything she felt was controlled by this man.

Her body spun higher and higher, her excitement out of control, until she gave a sharp cry and tumbled off the edge into a climax so intense that her mind blanked. She dug her nails hard into the hard muscle of his sleek, bronzed shoulders as her world shattered around her and her body tightened around his.

'I can feel that,' he groaned, and then he surged into her for a final time, his climax driving her straight back into another orgasm.

When the stars finally stopped exploding in her head, she opened her eyes and pressed her lips against his satin-smooth skin, desperately conscious that she'd succumbed to him yet again.

'That,' Casper murmured huskily, 'Was amazing.' Clearly in no hurry to move, he stroked her hair away from her face and stared into her eyes with a warmth that she hadn't seen before. 'Now, where were we in our conversation? I've lost track.'

Appalled at her own weakness, Holly closed her eyes. 'I was about to kick you but the baby did it for me.'

'You were about to forgive me,' Casper said confidently, and she opened her eyes and looked up at him.

'So is that what it was all about this time? Apology sex?'

Casper didn't answer for a moment, his hand unsteady as he stroked her hair away from her face. 'It was love sex, *tesoro*,' he said huskily, and Holly stilled.

It was like seeing a shimmer of water in the desert.

Real or a mirage?

'Love sex?' She was almost afraid to say the words. 'What do you mean, "love sex"?'

'I mean that I love you.'

Her heart was thudding. 'You told me that you weren't capable of love.'

'I was wrong. And I was trying to show you I was wrong. I think I express myself better physically than verbally.' His eyes gleamed with self-mockery. 'I was always better at maths than English. I'm the cold, analytical type, remember?'

A warm feeling spread through Holly's limbs and she started to tremble. 'Actually, that isn't true,' she said gently. 'You're very good with words.'

'But hopeless at matching them to the right emotion, if my lack of success at an apology is anything to go by.' Gently, he stroked a hand over her cheek. 'I love you, Holly. I think I loved you from the first moment I saw you. You were warm, gorgeous, sexy.' His eyes flickered to her mouth. 'You were *so* sexy I couldn't keep my hands off you.'

'And the moment we'd had sex, you wanted me to leave. Stop dressing it up, Casper. I'm not stupid.'

'I am the one who has been stupid,' he confessed in a raw tone. 'Stupid for not seeing what was under my nose. When we had sex the day of the rugby, I didn't know what had happened. I was living this crazy, cold, empty existence, and suddenly there you were. I was shocked by how I felt about you. I actually did think that you were different—and then you kissed me in the window.'

'You thought I'd done it for a photo opportunity.'

'Yes.' He didn't shrink from the truth. 'That is what I thought. And everything that happened after that seemed to back up my suspicions. You hid from the world and then announced that you were pregnant. It seemed to me that you were trying to make maximum impact from the story.'

'From your description, I should obviously be considering a career in public relations.'

'You have to understand that, when you're in the public eye, these things happen. You grow to expect them.' Casper drew away from her and sat up, his gaze thoughtful. 'Women have always wanted me for what I can give them. Even Antonia, who I thought loved me.'

Holly pulled a face. 'Yes, well, I can see why your experience with her made you very suspicious of women. I'm not stupid.'

'No, you're certainly not. And I'm not blaming Antonia. The blame lies entirely with myself.' Casper's admission was delivered with uncharacteristic self-deprecation. 'I allowed myself to see only bad in women, I expected only bad from women. And the chances of you having become pregnant on that one single occasion when I'd been told I was infertile—to have believed your story would have required a better man than me.'

'You're obviously super-fertile.'

He gave an aggressively masculine smile. 'So it would seem. And now I need to ask you something.' The smile faded and there was an unusual vulnerability in his dark eyes. 'Do you still love me? *Can* you still love me? You haven't said those words for a long time.'

Holly swallowed, her heart thudding hard. 'You didn't want to hear them,' she whispered. 'When I said them, or when I showed affection, you backed off. I didn't want to scare you away.'

'I taught myself to block out emotion because it was the only way I could survive,' Casper said roughly, leaning forwards and cupping her face in his hands. 'And I'm still waiting for you to answer my question.'

'I'm scared even to say the words,' she admitted with a strangled laugh. 'In case the whole bubble pops.'

'Say you can still love me, Holly. I need to hear you say it.'

'I never stopped loving you,' she said softly. 'I just stopped saying it because it upset you. That's another thing that "I love you" means to me. It means for ever. True love isn't something you can switch on and off, Casper. It's always there, sometimes when you'd rather it wasn't.'

Casper's breathing fractured, and he hauled her into his arms and held her tightly. 'Don't say that, because it reminds me how much I hurt you, and you have no idea how guilty I feel. You must have felt so alone, but I swear to you that you will never feel alone again.'

'I don't want you to feel guilty. I love you so much.'

'I don't deserve you.'

'You might well be saying that to yourself when I'm singing in the shower,' Holly joked feebly, and his grip tightened.

'After the way I behaved, most women would have walked away. I was so afraid you would do the same.'

'I would never do that.'

'No.' He withdrew slightly and stroked her cheek gently. 'You have an exceptionally lovely nature. You are kind, tolerant and forgiving. You have tremendous strength, and I truly admire your single-minded determination to do the very best for our baby. And our baby is so lucky to have you as a mother,' he murmured, pulling her against him again with firm, possessive hands.

Holly buried her face in his shoulder. 'I was terrified that you wouldn't love the baby.'

'And I was terrified to open up enough to love anything, because I saw love as a source of pain.'

'I know.' Holly touched his face. 'You were so wounded. I always knew that, and when we got together I told myself that, as long as I was patient, you would heal. I was so sure that everything would turn out all right, but I couldn't get through to you. I couldn't find the answer.'

'You were the answer.' Casper lifted her chin and silenced her fears with a possessive kiss. 'There will be no more problems between us. Ever.'

'Are you kidding?' Half laughing, half crying, Holly shook her head. 'You are stubborn, arrogant and used to getting your own way. How can we not have problems?'

'Because you are kind, tolerant and you adore me.' Casper, looking too gorgeous for his own good with roughened dark hair and the beginnings of stubble grazing his jaw, snuggled her against him again. 'And you have reminded me what true love really is.' His hand rested protectively on her rounded abdomen and his voice was suddenly husky. 'I never thought I believed in fairy tales, but this baby has changed my mind. I have great wealth and privilege, but the one thing I never thought I'd have is a family. You've given me that.'

Holly glanced up at him and then towards the fairy tale turrets of Santallia Palace in the distance. 'A family.' She savoured the word, and then smiled up at him, everything she felt shining in her eyes. 'That sounds like a very happy ending to me.'

* * * * *

*Harlequin is 60 years old,
and Harlequin Blaze is celebrating!
After all, a lot can happen in 60 years,
or 60 minutes…or 60 seconds!
Find out what's going down in Blaze's
heart-stopping new mini-series,*
FROM 0 TO 60!
*Getting from "Hello" to "How was it?"
can happen fast….*

Here's a sneak peek of the first book,
A LONG HARD RIDE
by Alison Kent
Available March 2009

"Is THAT FOR ME?" Trey asked.

Cardin Worth cocked her head to the side and considered how much better the day already seemed. "Good morning to you, too."

When she didn't hold out the second cup of coffee for him to take, he came closer. She sipped from her heavy white mug, hiding her grin and her giddy rush of nerves behind it.

But when he stopped in front of her, she made the mistake of lowering her gaze from his face to the exposed strip of his chest. It was either give him his cup of coffee or bury her nose against him and breathe in. She remembered so clearly how he smelled. How he tasted.

She gave him his coffee.

After taking a quick gulp, he smiled and said, "Good morning, Cardin. I hope the floor wasn't too hard for you."

The hardness of the floor hadn't been the problem. She shook her head. "Are you kidding? I slept like a baby, swaddled in my sleeping bag."

"In my sleeping bag, you mean."

If he wanted to get technical, yeah. "Thanks for the loaner. It made sleeping on the floor almost bearable." As had the warmth of his spooned body, she thought, then quickly changed the subject. "I saw you have a loaf of bread and some eggs. Would you like me to cook breakfast?"

He lowered his coffee mug slowly, his gaze as warm as the sun on her shoulders, as the ceramic heating her hands. "I didn't bring you out here to wait on me."

"You didn't bring me out here at all. I volunteered to come."

"To help me get ready for the race. Not to serve me."

"It's just breakfast, Trey. And coffee." Even if last night it had been more. Even if the way he was looking at her made her want to climb back into that sleeping bag. "I work much better when my stomach's not growling. I thought it might be the same for you."

"It is, but I'll cook. You made the coffee."

"That's because I can't work at all without caffeine."

"If I'd known that, I would've put on a pot as soon I got up."

"What time *did* you get up?" Judging by the sun's position, she swore it couldn't be any later than seven now. And, yeah, they'd agreed to start working at six.

"Maybe four?" he guessed, giving her a lazy smile.

"But it was almost two…" She let the sentence dangle, finishing the thought privately. She was quite sure he knew exactly what time they'd finally fallen asleep after he'd made love to her.

The question facing her now was where did this relationship—if you could even call it *that*—go from here?

* * * * *

Cardin and Trey are about to find out that
great sex is only the beginning....
Don't miss the fireworks!
Get ready for
A LONG HARD RIDE
by Alison Kent
Available March 2009,
wherever Blaze books are sold.

HARLEQUIN *Presents*

✦ ONE NIGHT BABY ✦

When passion leads to pregnancy!

PLEASURE, PREGNANCY AND A PROPOSITION
by Heidi Rice

With tall, sexy, gorgeous men like these,
it's easy to get carried away with
the passion of the moment—and end up
unexpectedly, accidentally, shockingly

PREGNANT!

Book #2809

Available March 2009

Don't miss any books in this exciting new
miniseries from Harlequin Presents!

HARLEQUIN *Presents*

International Billionaires

Life is a game of power and pleasure.
And these men play to win!

AT THE ARGENTINIAN
BILLIONAIRE'S BIDDING
by *India Grey*

Billionaire Alejandro D'Arienzo desires revenge
on Tamsin—the heiress who wrecked his past.
Tamsin is shocked when Alejandro threatens her
business with his ultimatum: *her name in tatters*
or her body in his bed…
Book #2806

Available March 2009

Eight volumes in all to collect!

HARLEQUIN Presents

EXTRA

THE BILLIONAIRE'S CONVENIENT WIFE

Forced to the altar for a marriage of convenience!

He's superrich, broodingly handsome and
needs a bride in name only....

She's innocent yet defiant, and she's about to be
promoted from mistress to convenient wife!

Look for all of our exciting books in March:

The Italian's Ruthless
Marriage Bargain #45
by KIM LAWRENCE

The Billionaire's
Blackmail Bargain #46
by MARGARET MAYO

The Billionaire's
Marriage Mission #47
by HELEN BROOKS

Jonas Berkeley's
Defiant Wife #48
by AMANDA BROWNING

www.eHarlequin.com

HPE0309

REQUEST YOUR FREE BOOKS!

HARLEQUIN *Presents* ®

PASSION GUARANTEED SEDUCTION

2 FREE NOVELS
PLUS 2
FREE GIFTS!

YES! Please send me 2 FREE Harlequin Presents® novels and my 2 FREE gifts (gifts are worth about $10). After receiving them, if I don't wish to receive any more books, I can return the shipping statement marked "cancel". If I don't cancel, I will receive 6 brand-new novels every month and be billed just $4.05 per book in the U.S. or $4.74 per book in Canada, plus 25¢ shipping and handling per book and applicable taxes, if any*. That's a savings of close to 15% off the cover price! I understand that accepting the 2 free books and gifts places me under no obligation to buy anything. I can always return a shipment and cancel at any time. Even if I never buy another book, the two free books and gifts are mine to keep forever.

106 HDN ERRW 306 HDN ERRL

Name	(PLEASE PRINT)	
Address		Apt. #
City	State/Prov.	Zip/Postal Code

Signature (if under 18, a parent or guardian must sign)

Mail to the **Harlequin Reader Service:**
IN U.S.A.: P.O. Box 1867, Buffalo, NY 14240-1867
IN CANADA: P.O. Box 609, Fort Erie, Ontario L2A 5X3

Not valid to current subscribers of Harlequin Presents books.

Want to try two free books from another line?
Call 1-800-873-8635 or visit www.morefreebooks.com.

* Terms and prices subject to change without notice. N.Y. residents add applicable sales tax. Canadian residents will be charged applicable provincial taxes and GST. Offer not valid in Quebec. This offer is limited to one order per household. All orders subject to approval. Credit or debit balances in a customer's account(s) may be offset by any other outstanding balance owed by or to the customer. Please allow 4 to 6 weeks for delivery. Offer available while quantities last.

Your Privacy: Harlequin Books is committed to protecting your privacy. Our Privacy Policy is available online at www.eHarlequin.com or upon request from the Reader Service. From time to time we make our lists of customers available to reputable third parties who may have a product or service of interest to you. If you would prefer we not share your name and address, please check here. ☐

HP08R

I ♥

HARLEQUIN *Presents*

BROUGHT TO YOU BY FANS OF HARLEQUIN PRESENTS.

We are its editors and authors and biggest fans—and we'd love to hear from YOU!

Subscribe today to our online blog at
www.iheartpresents.com

You're invited to join our Tell Harlequin Reader Panel!

By joining our new reader panel you will:

- Receive Harlequin® books—they are FREE and yours to keep with no obligation to purchase anything!
- Participate in fun online surveys
- Exchange opinions and ideas with women just like you
- Have a say in our new book ideas and help us publish the best in women's fiction

In addition, you will have a chance to win great prizes and receive special gifts!
See Web site for details. Some conditions apply.
Space is limited.

To join, visit us at
www.TellHarlequin.com.

THBPA0108